# MEMO FROM THE DEVIL

## SATAN'S STRATEGIC PREPARATIONS FOR
## THE END OF THE AGE

## BART BEVERS

WESTBOW
PRESS
A DIVISION OF THOMAS NELSON

Unless otherwise noted, scripture taken from the HOLY BIBLE, NEW INTERNATIONAL VERSION. © 1973, 1978, 1984, by International Bible Society. Used by permission of Zondervan. All rights reserved.
Scripture quotations marked NAS are taken from the New American Standard Bible, © 1960, 1962, 1963, 1968, 1971, 1972, 1973, 1975, and 1977, The Lockman Foundation, La Habra Calif. Used by permission.
All scripture quotations marked KJV are taken from the King James Version.
Scripture quotations marked "NKJV™" are taken from the New King James Version®. Copyright © 1982 by Thomas Nelson, Inc. Used by permission. All rights reserved.
All emphasized scripture is placed there by the author and is not emphasized in the original text.

WestBow Press books may be ordered through booksellers or by contacting:

WestBow Press
A Division of Thomas Nelson
1663 Liberty Drive
Bloomington, IN 47403
www.westbowpress.com
1-(866) 928-1240

Because of the dynamic nature of the Internet, any web addresses or links contained in this book may have changed since publication and may no longer be valid. The views expressed in this work are solely those of the author and do not necessarily reflect the views of the publisher, and the publisher hereby disclaims any responsibility for them.

ISBN: 978-1-4497-2974-5 (sc)
ISBN: 978-1-4497-2975-2 (hc)
ISBN: 978-1-4497-2973-8 (e)

Library of Congress Control Number: 2011918767

Printed in the United States of America

WestBow Press rev. date: 10/28/2011

# TABLE OF CONTENTS

# LIST OF TABLES AND CHAPTERS

For my parents, Frank and Shirley Bevers, who pointed us to Jesus Christ and led by example.

And for my wife Gina and our two children, who make life worth living.

"Few are those who see with their own eyes and feel with their own hearts."

Albert Einstein

# PREFACE

Most of the last twenty-three years, I have spent working in the fraud industry. Initially I worked for the federal government closing banks and savings and loans that committed fraud, and liquidating their remaining assets. After law school I spent almost ten years as an assistant district attorney focusing on fraud and white collar crime. Later I spent seven years working with the Office of Inspector General in Texas fighting fraud. Needless to say, I have seen a multitude of fraudulent acts committed and, unfortunately, the consequences which flow from those fraudulent acts.

Fraud is an intentional deception or intentional misrepresentation made by someone with knowledge that the lie they just engaged in will likely result in their unjustly receiving something of value (*usually money or property*). In the physical world fraud is costly. In the spiritual realm it is deadly—and Satan is good at it.

My motivation in writing this book is to expose some of the fraud that is being perpetrated against the human race, and especially the fraud being perpetrated against the body of Christ with two resulting outcomes. First, I hope that people will begin to *fear God* which means to take him seriously. Secondly, I hope that people will *obey God* which means to do what he says. As a trial attorney we have a saying called, *"stealing someone's thunder."* This strategy is utilized during a trial where one side discloses information before the other side does—in hopes of mitigating the potential impact of merely waiting until the other side introduces damaging evidence that you know they possess and intend to introduce. I hope this book opens your eyes and steals Satan's thunder. Satan has a strategy that he is actively working even as you read this sentence.

God and Satan are real beings. They really do exist. In the near future everyone on this planet is going to come to this understanding. We can either accept the free gift of grace that God has offered us through his son Jesus Christ by confessing with our mouths and believing in our hearts that God raised Jesus from the grave; or we can reject his gracious offer, live our lives the way we want and experience the horrific consequences that are just around the corner. My hope and prayer is that God will use this book to move people from where they are to the foot of the cross.

In the past I launched a website (www.give-an-answer. com) to further my efforts in sharing the gospel and equipping other Christ followers to do the same. Whether you are a Christ follower or someone who has rejected Christ—my prayer is that the Holy Spirit will somehow use this book to accomplish his will for your life. God's invitation to come out of the spectator stands and onto the playing field is open to everyone. The spectator stands are filled with armchair quarterbacks. Regrettably, the sidelines are crowded with Christians doing things their own way, not God's way. The joy you so desperately seek can only be found on the playing field. Put your seat cushion down and come join us on the field. If you want something you've never had, you must do something you've never done. Get into the game.

Do not be another one of Satan's victims. You were born with a will and the power to make choices. Choose God and avoid what is about to occur to the world. If you reject God's offer of salvation or merely wait too long to decide, you will experience a *parade of horribles* that your mind cannot even conceive. That is as clear as I know how to say it.

# INTRODUCTION

I'll never forget the day I first heard about the movie, *Dirty Harry*. I was eight years old and was not allowed to watch R-rated movies; however, my friends who did told me about the detective who was hunting a serial killer who killed people and taunted police by writing letters to local newspapers. It sounded interesting. When I found out the entire story was based on a real-life serial killer (*The Zodiac Killer in San Francisco*) something triggered inside me. What transpired in the real world was worse than in the movie, and it was real.

I could not believe that someone would kill defenseless people for fun and taunt the police who never solved the case or even arrested him. At eight years of age it was no longer the movie that piqued my interest, but the real-life perpetrators of crimes. Forty years later, the Zodiac investigations are still unsolved and all but one of the cryptographic ciphers the Zodiac mailed are still encrypted. This circumstance in life pushed me over the edge of decision. As a mere child, I knew deep down that I would someday be involved in the administration of criminal justice.

I never chose fraud, it always chose me. In sixth grade when an item turned up missing in our elementary school classroom and foul play was suspected, my teacher (*Mrs. Powell*) didn't go to the principal, she came to me for some reason I still do not understand. She told me that she knew I could figure it out and have the item returned to its rightful owner. It took a few days but she was right. I remember enjoying the process of investigating a criminal act. It felt as though this was what I was supposed to do. When I got older and realized the Holy Spirit had given me the spiritual gifts of *discernment, mercy,* and *teaching* I began to see the larger picture with more clarity. One of the reasons God put me here on earth was to help people with those spiritually-endowed gifts.

As a young prosecutor I prosecuted rapists, murderers, and child-molesters. However, what really piqued my interest were the smart criminals—the perpetrators of fraud. These were the well-dressed, subtle, seemingly unnoticeable, deceitful suspects with advanced college degrees whose outward polished veneer gave little indication of their true behaviors. From sixth grade on, the world of fraud continued to beckon me with repeated unsolicited invitations.

The only way to stop fraud (*criminal fraud or spiritual fraud*) is to prevent it from occurring. Several months ago I was training 200 staffers at the Capitol on "fraud awareness and prevention." I told them what I tell others—due to our *wills, consciences, minds,* and *emotions,* fraud prevention is oftentimes impossible. However, that does not absolve us from the responsibility of pursuing the objective of fraud prevention. The biggest obstacle to fraud prevention is the human heart. As the prophet Jeremiah stated, "*The heart is deceitful above all things*" (17:19 KJV).

Most every week I spend time in maximum security prisons sharing the gospel with unbelievers and studying the Bible with fellow believers who are imprisoned. Many of my *brothers in white* are no different than me or any other law-abiding citizen. Many of them made just one mistake and they happened to have been caught. The Holy Spirit has guided me to get involved with ministering to incarcerated men. Most of these men will get released someday. Their success upon release will hinge on their spiritual preparedness. Fraud prevention is not just a passion; it is also a way of life for some of us.

Digging into the Bible and searching for truth in prophetic scriptures is a challenge. Chuck Swindoll said it best on a recent radio program in 2011. Mr. Swindoll gave four guidelines to pursuing what truth is revealed in prophetic scriptures. They are:

1. *"While some things are revealed, much remains a mystery. It is a mark of immaturity to read more into the biblical text than it states. Be careful. Live comfortably with big chunks of the future remaining a mystery.*
2. *When searching for answers leave a lot of room for questions.*
3. *As you stand firm, be patient and tolerant with those who do not.*
4. *Though no one knows all the details don't hesitate to stand firm on the things that are clearly revealed."*

Charles R. Swindoll, Insight for Living, *The Day of the Lord*, April 27-28, 2011.

It was with these boundaries in mind that I wrote *Memo from the Devil*. Satan invented lying and he was a murderer from the beginning. Satan's fraudulent schemes are always laced with just enough truth to be palpable. Exposing his schemes (*spiritual fraud prevention*) is something only God can do. It is a mistake for anyone to underestimate Satan's extreme hatred of humanity or his 24/7/365 diligence. Fraud prevention necessitates pursuing the understanding of how perpetrators think and how they perceive reality. Peering into the mind of the *father of lies* is even more daunting; however, if we never ponder *why he does what he does,* we will always be behind the curve with respect to spiritual fraud prevention. While *Memo from the Devil* is a non-fictional work, it also contains a ten-part fictional memorandum written in the first person as though Satan is speaking to his demonic forces. The entire book is written from a premillennial, pre-tribulation perspective.

I hope *Memo from the Devil* pushes you over the edge of decision into a deeper walk with God. The Holy Spirit is very capable of bearing witness to any truths revealed in *Memo from the Devil.* My only advice is to seek God's counsel and follow his lead. This means taking God seriously and doing what he says. As I look back over the last forty years, I still remember that naïve, unsaved eight-year old boy who was exposed to a passion he did not fully understand. If I could, I would not say anything to him because he had to learn his lessons the hard way. His *failures,* not his *successes,* would shape him into the person he would become.

# CHAPTER ONE

## THE ORIGINS OF SIN

*By the abundance of your trade you were internally filled with violence, and you sinned; therefore I have cast you as profane from the mountain of God. And I have destroyed you, O covering cherub, from the midst of the stones of fire. Ezekiel 28:16 NAS*

# THE ORIGIN OF SIN IN HEAVEN:

Rebellion towards God began in heaven. In Ezekiel Chapter 28 the Bible uses two words to describe the "King of Tyre"[1] (*first "ruler" then "king"*). The second Hebrew word *melek* is used in the passage to describe "king." Ezekiel used the word sparingly. The only other time he used the word was in chapter 1 verse 2, when speaking of Israel's monarch King Jehoiachin. The change from using the word "ruler" to using the word "king" is significant.

Ezekiel described this "king" in terms that could not apply to a man. First, this "king" appeared in the Garden of Eden,[2] had been a guardian cherub,[3] had free access to God's holy mountain,[4] and was sinless from the time he was created.[5] Clearly Ezekiel was referring to Satan, the person behind the human king of Tyre. This was a dual reference to the human king of Tyre and the power behind him. Scripture supports this reference in other books of the Bible. Satan appeared in the Garden of Eden,[6] according to the Bible his chief sin was pride,[7] and he also had access to God's presence.[8]

Sin did not originate in the throne room of heaven instantaneously. There was a process that led to sin. It is that process that is described in detail in Ezekiel chapter 28. To fully understand what God refers to as "sin" we must analyze the process that led to its inception. This will provide us insight into how God evaluates the process of sin on human levels.

God described Satan as being created, beautiful, and perfect in beauty.[9] Satan walked in the midst of the stones of fire.[10] The Bible then says something incredibly important. The passage describes the specific activity in the process that led to the first sin. It describes what Satan was doing immediately prior to committing the first sin. The passage states, *"By the abundance of your trade, you were internally filled with violence."*[11] The Hebrew word translators used to describe "trade" is *raka*, which means *'to go about from one to another'*.[12] It was Satan's going about from one to another that led to his being internally being filled with violence.

Satan has continued this *"going about from one to another"* since the beginning. It is one of his trademarks because he still desires to be like God. In the book of Job God asked Satan from where he had come. Satan responded, *"From roaming about on the earth and walking around on it."*[13] The Bible also describes his activity as, *"prowling about like a roaring lion, seeking someone to devour."*[14] He is constantly on the move. In the human criminal vernacular it is his *modus operandi* (MO). One of Satan's distinguishing behavioral traits, is his *"going about from one to another."*

According to God's own words Satan was the most beautiful creature ever created because he was the only created being described in the Bible as being *"perfect in beauty."*[15] It is quite amusing that Satan is personified as a horned, red-tailed, pitchfork-bearing, impish figure. This is a far cry from God's description. A couple of things that probably motivated Satan at the time was when he began to notice (1) he was not omniscient and omnipresent like God, and (2) how incredibly beautiful he was. If you are not omniscient and omnipresent like God (*all-knowing and can be everywhere at once*) what can you do to try and keep up? Answer—increase your activity. The likely reason why Satan was rushing around to and fro is quite simply he wanted to be like God.[16] Satan decided he wanted to be like God and he wanted what God had. Some might say that he started to believe his own press. Satan may have walked about in heaven from one angelic being to another, while he heard compliments about his beauty and his privileges. He might have heard angels whispering about how they wish they were that beautiful. It's possible that he heard one too many compliments. Satan obviously realized the only persons more beautiful than himself were—the Father, Son, and the Holy Spirit. The Trinity is one God *revealed* in three persons.

Sin is Satan's goal. Sin is quite often the by-product of a series of decisions. These decisions are a process. Small decisions lead to larger decisions and the process builds upon itself until the series of wrong decisions produces the only thing disobedience can, quite simply sin. This violence turned into rebellion and Satan organized a *coup d'état,* which led to one-third of the angelic hosts being cast from heaven with him.[17]

# THE ORIGIN OF SIN ON PLANET EARTH:

I have often wondered over the years about why Satan did not choose a giraffe to approach Eve in the Garden of Eden. Surely a giraffe could keep an eye on virtually everything around. A giraffe would command your attention. There is no doubt that a giraffe could make a lasting impression on a much less imposing human being. However, the same could be said about a lion, gorilla, or rhinoceros. If you have ever wondered why Satan chose to appear as a serpent, it was because of its characteristics. God included this fact in the third chapter of Genesis.

In short, Satan chose the serpent because of its subtlety. Subtle means unnoticeable. Genesis states, "Now the serpent was more *subtle* than any beast of the field which the Lord God had made."[18] The Hebrew word *aruwm* (aw-room') is defined as 'cunning (*usually in a bad sense*), crafty, prudent, subtle'.[19] The word *aruwm* is the past participle of *aram (aw-ram)*, which means to be (*or make*) bare, but used only in the derivative sense (*through the idea perhaps of smoothness*).[20] The serpent could find its way anywhere. It was the most unnoticeable animal God had made. In serpentine form Satan did not have to approach anyone. He could lie in wait quietly and without bringing attention to himself. In the form of a serpent, he could patiently wait for the opportunity to strike up a conversation that seemed ever so subtle and innocently coincidental. Subtlety is effective, it works. If Satan had a motto it might be—never let 'em see you coming.

It is his subtleties that confuse Christ followers. Like one of my favorite songs by the Rolling Stones, "Sympathy for the Devil," states, "*What's puzzling you is the nature of my game*"[21] — a very accurate lyric. The very moment people look for obvious signs of evil, his subtlety strategy has accomplished its goal. For example, humans would never choose a short art student who was studying painting to lead the Nazi's into the Third

Reich and kill six million Jews, but Satan did. Humans would never choose a clean-cut father and son driving a family sedan to assassinate pedestrians in the Washington D.C. area, but Satan did. Satan chooses the unnoticeable and humans look for the obvious. It is a deadly combination. The world usually never sees him coming because they are looking for a *recognizable form of evil*, when that is exactly what he desires. Humans *should* pay very close attention to events that first appear as (1) subtle, (2) everyday, (3) unnoticeable, and (4) run-of-the-mill. Unfortunately, however we do not. As the old saying goes, *the devil is in the details.*

# MEMO FROM THE DEVIL:
## PART 1-INTRODUCTION

**TO:**          **All Demonic Forces Worldwide**

**FROM:**          **LUCIFER, Your Supreme Ruler and God**

**DATE:**          November 1, 2011

**SUBJECT:**          **PRIORITY ONE DIRECTIVES**

You will all be held accountable for reviewing, understanding, and following the directives contained within this message. Any failures on your part or deviations from my instructions will be dealt with severely. Questions should be addressed through your chain-of-command. I will begin by reminding you of our vision and mission.

**VISION STATEMENT:** We must exterminate the Jewish race of humans; thereby, making it impossible for God to fulfill his stated promises to the Jews. Once they are eradicated, he will be a proven liar and one of two things will occur. Either:

(1) He will suspend his sentence upon us to spend eternity in the lake of fire, or
(2) He will experience another rebellion in heaven as the remaining angels in heaven who witness his failed promises firsthand, rise up against him like we did not so long ago.

**MISSION STATEMENT:** Utilizing our primary tool of "fraud" (*intentional deceit or intentional misrepresentation*), **target the minds of unbelievers and Christ followers.** Lead them astray from the purity and simplicity of devotion to Jesus Christ. Minimize, mitigate, and neutralize the straightforwardness of the gospel message through every available means. Ensure that our counterfeit explanations are appealing, attractive, encouraging, caring, intelligent, and plausible.

# CHAPTER TWO

# BIBLICAL ESCHATOLOGY

*I am telling you now before it happens, so that when it does happen you will believe that I am who I am. Very truly I tell you, whoever accepts anyone I send accepts me; and whoever accepts me accepts the one who sent me. John 13:19-20*

# Premillennial, Amillennial, and Postmillennial Eschatological Interpretations:

There are three major viewpoints concerning the theology of end times. There is (1) premillennialism, (2) amillennialism and (3) postmillennialism. These are three major frameworks within the Christian realm. When I use the words "Christ follower" I am referring to those who *"have confessed with their mouth Jesus as Lord, and believed in their heart that God raised him from the dead."*[22] That is God's definition of a Christian. All three frameworks for interpreting certain prophecies from the Bible have three things in common. All three interpretations agree that (1) Christ will return, (2) Satan will be defeated, and (3) Christ will unite all believers.

Loraine Boettner describes **postmillennialism** as, *"That view of last things which holds that the kingdom of God is now being extended in the world through the preaching of the gospel and the saving work of the Holy Spirit in the hearts of individuals, that the world is eventually to be Christianized, and that the return of Christ will occur at the close of a long period of righteousness and peace commonly called the 'Millennium' . . . the second coming of Christ will be followed immediately by the general resurrection, the general judgment, and the introduction of heaven and hell in their fullness."*[23]

Charles Ryrie describes **amillennialism** as *"the view of last things that holds there will be no Millennium before the end of the world. Until the end there will be a parallel development of both good and evil, God's kingdom and Satan's. After the second coming of Christ at the end of the world there will be a general resurrection and general judgment of all people."*[24]

Ryrie also describes **premillennialism** as *"the view that the second coming of Christ will occur prior to the millennium which will see the establishment of Christ's kingdom on this earth for a literal 1,000 years. It also understands that there will be several occasions* *when resurrections and judgments will take place. Eternity will begin after the 1,000 years are concluded. Within premillennialism there are those who hold differing views as to the time of the Rapture."* [25]

The one-thousand-year millennium period is the time when the Bible describes Jesus reigning as King. The main difference between premillennialism and amillennialism focuses on the nature of the millennium. Premillennialists believe it is a literal thousand years while amillennialists believe it is a figurative length of time.

In short, premillennialism says that there is a future millennium[26] where Christ will rule and reign over the earth. It is predicted that at the beginning of the millennium Satan and his demonic forces will be bound and peace will exist on the entire earth. At the end of the thousand years Satan will be released in order to raise an army against Jesus. Jesus will throw Satan into the lake of fire forever and the final judgment will take place with the new heavens and the new earth being made.

Amillennialism is the teaching that there is no literal thousand-year reign of Christ as referenced in Revelation 20. It sees the thousand-year period spoken of in Revelation 20 as figurative. Instead, it supposes that we are in the millennium now, and that at the return of Christ,[27] there will be the final judgment and the heavens and the earth will then be destroyed and remade.[28]

Based upon my understanding of scripture the premillennial interpretation of the Bible is most accurate. Therefore, my analyses and conclusions are predicated upon this assumption. This book is also written from that perspective.

# MEMO FROM THE DEVIL:
## PART 2—RELIGIOUS TEACHINGS

### INVOLVING CHRIST FOLLOWING SHEPHERDS

I am pleased to report that our strategy towards Christ followers with respect to prophetic scriptures is working better than expected. Prophecy makes up twenty-seven percent of the Bible and less than one percent of the sermons preached from evangelical, born-again churches. That is beautiful!

Blind the Christ followers to the fact that their understanding of prophecy matters to God. You should whisper into the ears of Christ followers, *"It doesn't really matter whether you believe correctly or not."* Blind them to the reality that the Most High does care about their understanding of prophecy. Blind them to the fact that they are stewards of the mysteries of God and he always demands faithfulness of stewards.[29]

Make sure that Christian clergy fear that twenty-seven percent of the Bible. They should feel that it is too hard to understand. They should also feel that it is too frightful and time-consuming to tackle. When these fears give birth to permissiveness and ultimately rationalization, tell them it's OK. Make them feel justified about not comprehensively addressing this twenty-seven percent of the Bible. Make sure their wives enable these behaviors and perpetuate this cycle under the auspices of supporting their husbands. They're such damn hypocrites. They never fail to find some verses about giving, tithing, or helping out in the children's area of the church to guilt-trip their congregations into *manning the oars*. But they shudder in fear and lack of faith when they encounter something that is challenging. This is proof that people will go exactly where they are led to go. Make sure these clergy are surrounded by elders who are either (1) hand-picked by the senior pastor, (2) co-dependent, or (3) non-confrontational. The last thing we need are elders who ask tough questions. Be very sensitive to this phenomenon especially when a new cycle of elders is elected.

The beauty of this apostasy by church leaders is what comes out the other end—a malnourished, incomplete, uninformed body of believers. Do you see the similarities between the clergy who fail to address prophecy and the politicians? Good, I thought you would.

## In Other Religions

We should continue proliferating teachings in other religions similar to biblical prophecies so when the events occur there is something else to point to as "why the event occurred." We do not want the human race to experience events foretold centuries ago and realize they were predicted in the Bible. By way of example, after Noah survived the flood, we immediately influenced subsequent generations to believe that ancient Sumerian texts have an identical flood story that predated the actual flood. Another good example is the Mahdi (*Messiah figure*) and the Dajjal (*Antichrist figure*) in Islamic teachings. When I get ready to introduce these figures, it will be a far easier sale since we have laid the groundwork of deceit far in advance.

More specifically, the Bible predicts that the **antichrist** will be wounded with a sword in Zechariah 11 and Revelation 13. The Zechariah passage even states he will be blinded in his right eye. Because of this we ensured the **antichrist figure** in Islamic teachings (*the Ad-Dajjal*) would be blinded in the right eye and that his eye would look like a bulging grape. As you should know, this reference comes from the Sahih al-Bukhari, one of the six canonical hadith collections of Islam. In short, due to the proliferation of counterfeit teachings in other religions we will be able to point to sources outside the Bible to explain certain events.

# CHAPTER THREE

# THE POLITICAL WORLD

*For the time will come when people will not put up with sound doctrine. Instead, to suit their own desires, they will gather around them a great number of teachers to say what their itching ears want to hear. 2 Timothy 4:3*

# THE POLITICAL COSMOS:

Globally the political world is broad and diverse. Politics in a democratic form of government is extremely simple. It is not as complicated as we usually make it appear. With a democratic form of government, there are only two rules in politics.

Rule #1:    Get elected or get re-elected.
Rule #2:    Let's do what I want to do ("I" meaning the elected politician).

There is no rule #3. To properly understand a political issue in a democracy we must ask a question that is relevant and material to one or both of the aforementioned rules. **Relevancy** is defined as having *"any tendency to make the existence of any fact that is of consequence to the determination of the action more probable or less probable than it would be without the evidence."* **Materiality** is defined with eight words and is part of the previous definition: *"of consequence to the determination of the action."* When you are analyzing a political dilemma within a democracy, you must ask questions that are material to the two aforementioned rules. If your question is immaterial to these two rules, you are asking the wrong question. If you fail to follow these precepts you will incorrectly analyze the issue at hand. If your analysis is wrong then your strategy and behaviors designed to deal with that problem will also be wrong. You must ask the correct questions to arrive at an accurate analysis.

Also, behavior trumps words. Pay very little attention to what a politician **says** in public forums and pay very close attention to what he or she **does**. As a society we have not figured this out yet. Realistically I doubt that this *light bulb* will ever come on. Voters believe most of what they hear because politicians tell them what they want to hear. When subsequent behaviors are observed and they fail to align with previous statements, voters either forget what was said or they get too busy to do anything about it. Then comes a second round of political statements telling voters what they want to hear and the cycle continues.

We as voters are largely blind to the fact that we are responsible for the character of our executive, legislative, and judicial leaders. This blindness on our part yields recklessness, ignorance, and corruption every time. Therefore, it is the sheer tolerance of the masses that breeds the very corruption we loathe. Tolerance equals failure to control the political forums. We are deceived.

If voters chose to analyze political events with merely these two rules it would bring some level of clarity to most any political issue that concerned them. It would also make the enemy's job much more difficult.

Politics is all about relationships. In fact, the DNA of politics *is* relationships. If you looked at politics under a microscope you would only see relationships. When I visit a capitol building I'm always amused to experience the web of interconnectivity. It's almost like Hillbilly Heaven. In fact, you can almost hear the banjo music when you enter a capitol building. Every elected person's office is somehow connected to every other office. Senator X has a staffer who went to law school with Representative Y's Chief-of-Staff, and she is engaged to a guy whose sister is Governor Z's public policy wonk, etc. The people involved in politics are truly a web of interconnectivity. They collectively look at the world through one lens—politics.

The tragedy of this reality is they share a collective blind spot. Anything they hear from a trusted source becomes their reality. If a politician hears something from a trusted source (*i.e. someone they know*), they will believe anything they hear. Whatever they heard gets stuck in their heads and becomes their truth. Politicians are very different from most other people who know there are always at least two sides to a story.

Because of this political blind spot the most effective political strategy that can be employed is *"beat em' downtown."* For example, if Person A and Person B have adverse political interests on an issue, the first person to reach the capitol and tell his version of the story will win ninety-five percent of the time.

Regardless of the truth, when someone has important political interests at stake, the most effective strategy to get what they want is to ensure their version of the story is the first version told at the capitol. This strategy has worked for centuries and will likely continue to work if employed.

The Bible teaches us that one of our three primary enemies is the *cosmos*.[30] The *cosmos* or "the world" as it is sometimes known is the world system organized and operated by Satan which opposes and excludes God. This counterfeited rival system operates 24/7. All you need to do to witness this system in action is to turn on your television. You will quickly begin to learn how you are supposed to look and what car you are supposed to drive.

Bible dictionaries should have a picture of a capitol building next to the definition of *cosmos*. Our political system in the United States is a perfect example of the *cosmos* in action. It is a microcosm of the cosmos. There are always good Christian people who work within the political system. However, in my experience many of these Christians also worship at the altar of the *cosmos*. Many Christians within the political system simply do not stand out. Their identity as a Christ follower often takes a backseat to their identity within the system. They are trained not to challenge the system, to accept it and be a part of it. The system itself will train people accordingly. Many Christians within the political system tend to accept and embrace the system and forget God's warning in 1 John 2:15-17 that this entire system is headed for the holy shredder.

The *sugar* of the cosmos system is the constant, subtle message that you can be on the throne of your own life. You are number one, not God. This explains why the two rules of politics exist and operate so smoothly within the *cosmos* system. It's all about me. How can I get re-elected and do what I want to do? Me, me, me—it's all about me.

When you get near the political system; pay attention to the pronouns that are used in conversation. "I" and "me" are very popular. Also pay attention to what is not said. Rarely is God's will discussed or contemplated. Effectual fervent prayer seeking God's will is even rarer.

The biggest mistake Christ followers make in regards to the political system is we are not fruit inspectors. The Bible teaches us to be fruit inspectors.[31] If someone tells you they are an apple tree and you never see any apples, they may not be an apple tree. My advice to Christians regarding politics mirrors what I will tell my 3-year old daughter when she is ready to start dating boys—pay little attention to what they say and pay very close attention to what they do.

Many people (*Christ followers included*) truly doubt the existence of our three enemies; *Satan, human depravity* and the *cosmos*. If you are included in this group of doubters I have a suggestion for you. Spend thirty minutes a day for one month, praying for God to tear down the ungodly strongholds within our political system. In less than one week you will find yourself standing right next to the enemy as you become the focus of his attention. I have tried this exercise several times and have never made it to day thirty.

# MEMO FROM THE DEVIL: PART 3 — POLITICS

As you know, all humans (*Christ followers and unbelievers*) have three enemies:

(1) me,
(2) human depravity [*a.k.a. the flesh*], and
(3) the world [*i.e . . . the "cosmos" world system we operate which excludes God*].

All three enemies operate 24/7 and the last two run for the most part on autopilot. Leverage these weapons at your disposal within every political realm. The aggregate impact of your synergistic efforts should always leverage these three weapons by utilizing our three primary strategies; the lust of the flesh, the lust of the eyes and the boastful pride of life.

Targeting the minds of people is a very simple iterative process. The process is look ⇨ think ⇨ meditate ⇨ actions ⇨ habits ⇨ character ⇨ destiny. What people look at they think about. What they think about they meditate on. What they meditate on they act on. Habits are then formed which molds character and ultimately their destiny. This mind-targeting is an integral component of all three aforementioned strategies.

The Christ followers within the political machines we operate are our biggest concern. Keep them busy. Make sure we mitigate their impact by bombarding them with some simple messages on a recurring basis. Ensure that they believe compromising is part of their job. Once they accept this premise they become benign. If you become aware of prayer and fasting, deal with it immediately. Keep them away from their Bibles. If you encounter any Christ followers who study the Bible regularly make sure they believe that Bible study for studies sake is the goal. DO NOT allow them to realize that God's goal for Bible study is life-change. I'm OK with the Bible study nerds as long as they don't start applying what they have read. If you witness any Christ followers attempting to act on what they've learned, turn up the heat until they backslide back to where they were.

Never forget when shaping human behavior that positive reinforcement (*adding something in order to increase a response*) is most effective. Humans are animals and this works on them just as well as adding a treat to increase the response of a dog sitting upon command. Just remember *praise and rewards* when you see the response we desire. When utilizing positive reinforcement always use variable schedules. More specifically, variable ratio schedules of applying the reinforcer after a variable number of responses; and variable interval schedules of applying the reinforcer after a *variable* amount of time. These two schedules are the most effective methods of applying positive reinforcement.

There should be no conversations in the political realms involving consequences or judgment. People do not want to hear about those two topics, so give them what their itching ears want to hear. On that note, do not allow Christ followers outside the political circles to realize our biggest concern in democracies—their voting power. We have successfully indoctrinated Christ followers into believing what they hear from lawmakers. Just make sure politicians sprinkle enough religious lingo into their words to give the appearance that they are true believers. The last thing we need now is for Christ followers to start inspecting the fruit of lawmakers' lives.

Never forget the importance of *controlling the message*. Do what you have to do within the media to accomplish this goal. As long as we frame the issues we will get the desired result. Be extremely wary of Christ followers who engage in independent issue formulation. Remember, he who frames the issue wins the argument.

Our *cosmos* world system has something for everybody. Never forget that. Ensure everyone within political circles

(*Christ followers and unbelievers alike*) pursue what they desire. Find out what they desire and lead them where we want them to go with the aforementioned positive reinforcement/variable schedule techniques. Thankfully no one (*Christ followers nor unbelievers*) takes God seriously anymore.

# CHAPTER FOUR

# SIGNS OF THE COMING APOCALYPSE

*So be on your guard, I have told you everything ahead of time. Even so, you see these things happening, you know that it is near, right at the door . . . What I say to you, I say to everyone: Watch!. Mark 13:23,29,37 NIV*

# SIGNS OF THE COMING APOCALYPSE:

There are two general points of reference we can look to in discerning when the second coming will occur. First we can look to the signs Jesus gave in Matthew 24, Mark 13, and Luke 21. Secondly, we can look to the chronological series of seals, trumpets, and bowls (vials) judgments described in Revelation 6:1 through 16:21 (*which only begin after the seven-year tribulation has already begun*).

From the perspective of an American citizen, the best way to analyze this is to look at the second coming like Christmas and the rapture like Thanksgiving. When you walk into a shopping mall the day after Halloween you always see Christmas decorations in the mall. You see Christmas decorations in the mall—and it isn't even Thanksgiving. If you see Christmas decorations signifying that Christmas is approaching then Thanksgiving must be even closer. If you see prophetic signs signifying that the second coming is approaching then the rapture must be even closer. I'll discuss this distinction in more detail below.

Jesus, himself compared the signs of the coming judgments and the apocalypse to the birth pains of a woman.[32] In essence they will increase in frequency and intensity as the time approaches. We may not be able to determine the day or the hour,[33] but we can certainly determine when it is getting close—and that time is now. Since Jesus used the analogy of labor pains, let's take a look at the parallels.

For us as human beings, "labor" (*or birth pains*) generally requires timing the contractions from the onset of one to the onset of the next. If the birth pains last at least one minute (*contraction*), and have been occurring every five minutes (*frequency*) for the last hour (*period of time*), the patient is generally considered to be in a *de facto* state of labor. For example, a patient who has a 1 minute labor pain (*contraction*), every 5 minutes (*frequency*), for a period of 60 minutes (*period of time*) is in labor. Statistically speaking those variables could be expressed in a formula as $(Ct + 4(Ct) \geq 60)$. [Ct = contraction, 4(Ct) = frequency, 60 = number of minutes]. Therefore, the first contraction would be expressed as $1 + 4(1) = 5$, the second contraction would be $2 + 4(2) = 10$ and so on until you get to the last contraction in the 60-minute time period which would be the twelfth contraction or $12 + 4(12) = 60$. Using the formulaic model of $(Ct + 4(Ct) \geq 60)$, we can ascertain the general onset of labor pains, or in this case the beginning of the tribulation period and therefore the earlier event (*the rapture*). Simply plug in the biblically predicted events as contractions and do the math. This is why I feel we are getting close to Christ's return. I can say it is imminent but I cannot say it is soon.

Do not bother trying to predict a specific date because it is a waste of time and resources. I believe God did this on purpose. The four major events in a human pregnancy are (1) conception, (2) gestation period, (3) labor, and (4) birth. Based upon the metaphor Jesus used, these can be paralleled to the four material events in biblical eschatology, (1) Pentecost, (2) church age, (3) seven-year tribulation period, and (4) the second coming. When we utilize the formulaic model of $(Ct + 4(Ct) \geq 60)$ in the context of the above parallels (1) conception = Pentecost, (2) gestation period = church age, (3) labor = seven-year tribulation period, and (4) birth = the second coming—it doesn't really matter what data you plug in. Any relevant data we choose to plug into the formula as "contractions" provide the answer—we are getting closer than ever. **It is a complete waste of time to try to predict exact dates when it is impossible to do so.** Imminent means it could happen at any moment; however, we cannot say it will happen soon. It is disturbing to read the number of media stories of people who are deceived into believing that they can predict specific dates. Every time someone is deceived into setting dates, and the event fails to occur it damages the credibility of biblical prophecy in the minds of unbelievers and Christ followers alike.

# MEMO FROM THE DEVIL:
## PART 4 — SIGNS OF THE END TIMES

### ASTEROIDS AND COMETS

As you may know, international space administration officials routinely scan the skies for asteroids or comets that may be an impact threat to Earth. They want to be apprised of any potential significant impacts before they occur.

Asteroid 1999 RQ36: Has a 1-in-1,000 chance of striking Earth in 2182. That impact would likely not be small, since the asteroid has a size of 579 meters—as big as six football fields.

Asteroid 2010 AL30: In January of 2011, passed within about 80,000 miles of Earth. However, 2010 AL30 was merely 11 meters wide.

Asteroid Apophis: will come very close to the Earth on or about April 13, 2036. Scientists predict that it will pass approximately 18,300 miles from Earth. Apophis is larger than 200 meters, which is not big enough to create global devastation.

**What human scientists have failed to explain to the world is that the real concern are comets not asteroids.** *Asteroids* typically maintain easily identifiable orbits between Mars and Jupiter. *Comets*, however, unlike asteroids, are hidden in the remote reaches of the solar system. Humans usually learn about comets shortly before they pose a threat.

We have identified three significant comets that will impact the Earth in the imminent future. The first is likely the object identified in Revelation 8:8 (*the second trumpet judgment*) and it will hit the ocean. The second is likely "Wormwood" identified in Revelation 8:10 (*the third trumpet judgment*) and it will hit land. The third is a series of smaller comets—likely the objects identified in Revelation 16:21 (*The seventh vial judgment*), they are much smaller than the previous two and will break up as they hit what's left of the Earth's atmosphere, producing broken pieces weighing from 57 to 130 pounds each.[34]

As you know, the seven-year tribulation period will last 2,520 days (*seven lunar years*). Further, since the premillennial, pretribulational interpretation of scripture is likely the most accurate, you can do the math yourself. If the third aforementioned series of comets occurs just before the Battle of Armageddon, the beginning of the tribulation period and the rapture must be at least seven years earlier. Due to the distance, timing, orbits, relative size and anticipated impact dates of the three aforementioned celestial bodies, **I am moving our Readiness Mode to "IMMEDIATE" effective today**. You should operate as if the rapture could occur at any moment. Get your minds set for battle. We will capitalize on each and every tragedy coming upon the world. Mankind has never experienced the global unmitigated wrath from both me and the Most High at the same time.

## EARTHQUAKES

Based upon information collected by the United States Geological Survey (USGS),[35] we have also noticed the following trends in regards to major earthquakes. On a global scale, from 2002 through 2010, major earthquakes (*registering 5.0 or higher on the Richter scale*) have increased in frequency and intensity. Over this nine-year time period they have a relative increase in **frequency of 58.14 percent** with an accompanying increase in **intensity of 8.79 percent**. *SEE CHARTS—MAJOR EARTHQUAKES FROM 2002-2010.*

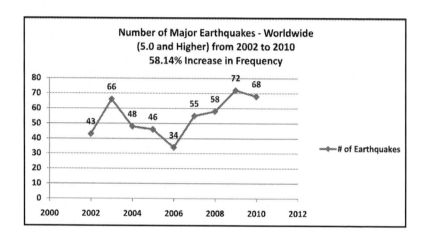

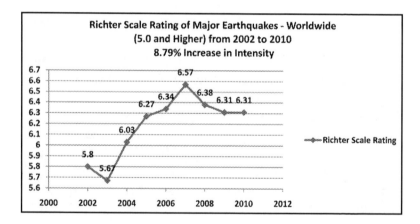

Chart 1: Major Earthquakes from 2002-2010

# CHAPTER FIVE

## THE RAPTURE VERSUS THE SECOND COMING

*As Jesus was sitting on the Mount of Olives, the disciples came to him privately. "Tell us," they said, "when will this happen, and what will be the sign of your coming and of the end of the age?" Jesus answered: "Watch out that no one deceives you. Matthew 24:3-4*

# INTRODUCTION

There are 810,697 words comprising 31,124 verses in the King James Version (KJV) of the Bible. Eight thousand, three hundred and fifty-two of those verses contain prophetic material. In essence, twenty-seven percent of the Bible is prophetic. Approximately half of those prophecies have already come true and the other half remains to be fulfilled. Two of the biggest events discussed in those prophecies are the rapture and the second coming.

# THE RAPTURE: 1 CORINTHIANS 15:51-52; 1 THESSALONIANS 4:13-17; JOHN 14:1-3

In John 14:1-3, Jesus made four promises. He said (1) in his father's house are many mansions; (2) he's going there to prepare a place for believers; (3) he's coming back, and (4) he will take believers with him so they can be together. The third and fourth promises are speaking to the rapture.

In 1 Corinthians 15:51-52 the Bible speaks of a mystery. More specifically it states, *"Listen, I tell you a mystery: We will not all sleep, but we will all be changed—in a flash, in the twinkling of an eye, at the last trumpet. For the trumpet will sound, the dead will be raised imperishable, and we will be changed."*

The "mystery" is not the resurrection. The *"mystery"* is— *not all Christ followers are going to die.* An entire generation of future or present Christ followers will be taken by Jesus into the sky in the twinkling of an eye. This is a mystery revealed in the New Testament but not the Old Testament. Similarly, the Old Testament predicted that a Messiah would come. The Old Testament did not reveal that the coming Messiah would be *God himself.* The incarnation of God coming to Earth in the form of a man still awes me.

Acts 1:9 and 11 document Jesus's ascension. They state, *"a cloud hid him from their sight . . . This same Jesus . . . will come back in the same way that you have seen him go into heaven."* Further, 1 Thessalonians 4:13-17 states,

> *Brothers and sisters, we do not want you to be uninformed about those who sleep in death, so that you do not grieve like the rest* [of mankind], *who have no hope. We believe that Jesus died and rose again, and so we believe that <u>God will bring with Jesus those who have fallen asleep in him</u>. According to the Lord's word, we tell you that we who are still alive, who are left till the coming of the Lord, will certainly not precede those who have fallen asleep. <u>For the Lord himself will come down from heaven, with a loud command, with the voice of the archangel and with the trumpet call of God, and the dead in Christ will rise first</u>.[7] After that, <u>we who are still alive and are left will be caught up together with them in the clouds to meet the Lord in the air</u>. And so we will be with the Lord forever.*

These three passages are clearly referring to a separate and distinct event. The rapture and the second coming are two different events separated by time. Chronologically, the rapture will occur first and then the second coming will occur.

## THE SECOND COMING: ZECHARIAH 14:1-11; REVELATION 19:11-16

Out of the Bible's 31,124 verses, 1,800 verses address the second coming of Jesus Christ. That is six percent of the entire Bible and approximately four percent of the New Testament addressing the second coming. The second coming is where Christ followers will witness Jesus Christ fight the final battle—Armageddon. Jesus will return to the Earth to judge and to set up his millennial reign.

Suffice it to say that these two events are clearly two different events separated by time. The following table addresses the distinctions. SEE CHART— COMPARING THE RAPTURE TO THE SECOND COMING.

| | RAPTURE (John 14:1-3; 1 Corinthians 15:50-58; *1 Thessalonians 4:13-18) | 2ND COMING (Zechariah 14:1-11; Revelation 19:11-16) |
|---|---|---|
| Geographical Area | Air: Meet the Lord in the air (1 Thess 4:17) take believers to heaven (John 14:2-3) | Mount of Olives: Christ descends on the Mount of Olives (Zech 14:3) |
| Who Removes People | Jesus Christ removes believers and takes them to heaven (1 Thess 4:16-17) [the dead will hear the voice of the Son of God — John 5:25] | Angels sent by God gather unbelievers, takes them to the fiery furnace (Matt 13:41; Matt 13:49, 50; Matt 24:37-39, 40-41) |
| Who is taken from the Earth and who is left? | -Christians taken from the earth -Unbelievers left on the earth (1 Thess 4:17) | -Unbelievers taken from earth to judgment -Christians are gathered and then left on earth for millennial reign(Matt 13:49-50) |
| Jesus' Coming — in relation to the 7-Year Tribulation | Before: Jesus comes before the hour of trial to rescue believers from it (1Thess 5:4, 9) | After: Jesus comes after the tribulation to -inflict final punishment, -conquer his enemies, and -begin his reign of world from Jerusalem (Matt 24:29-30) |
| Warning signs of the event indicating its approach? | No signs are given in scripture which must take place before the rapture (Phil 3:20; 1 Thess 1:10; Tit 2:13; Heb 9:28) | Detailed signs are given which must occur before Christ's 2nd Coming (Matt 24:4-28; Mark 13; Luke 21; Rev 19:11-21) |

| Judgment | Every scripture about the rapture **fails to mention trials or God's judgments** falling on the earth before the rapture occurs | Every scripture about the 2nd coming is set in the **context of tribulation & judgment** (Zech 14:1-2; 1 Thess 4:13-18; 1 Thess 5:4,9; 1 Thess 1:10; Rev 3:10,11; Matt 24:29,30) |
|---|---|---|
| **Difference in the timing of the resurrections predicted** | During: Resurrection of the dead in Christ occurs **during the descent of Christ**(1 Thess 4:13-18) | After: Resurrection of the righteous dead (who died during the tribulation) during the millennium occurs only **after Christ has descended to the earth** (Rev 19:11-21; Rev 20:1-8) |

**Chart 2: Comparison of the Rapture to the Second Coming**

# Memo from the Devil: Part 5 — December 21, 2012 and The war to Come

## December 21, 2012

As you know we spend at least fifty percent of our time waging the war of counter-intelligence and disinformation. We have been very successful with this strategy. The more time we can get people to run down *rabbit trails* that go nowhere the better. Every minute a human spends running down a *rabbit trail* that leads nowhere is a minute not spent pursuing the truth. The rapture of Christ followers is rapidly approaching and we must lay the psychological foundation of "why." We certainly do not want unbelievers who are left behind to ponder *Maybe all the people who disappeared in the twinkling of an eye were raptured by Jesus Christ as my Christian friends used to caution me about.* We must present a counterfeit psychological alternative (*i.e. aliens took them*) and we must lay the foundation NOW for that lie to sound believable.

The sun and planets only align with the center of the Milky Way galaxy once every 26,000 years and that alignment will occur on December 21, 2012. In short, the sun and all the planets in the solar system will align with the galactic equator (*i.e. the black hole in the center of this galaxy*) on that date. Based on my experience it should not cause much of anything. However, we must always think strategically and be prepared to offer a counterfeit alternative. Since the rapture of Christ followers is rapidly approaching, we might be able to use this interstellar event as part of our plan, should the rapture occur at any time in the foreseeable future. Not only that, but we can bootstrap other unrelated events to give the appearance that the end of the world as we know it was predicted by humans long ago, and it has no relation to biblical prophecies.

More specifically, the Mayan Long Count calendar is due to end on that same date. Many of us were present in the

Mayan culture when their calendar was developed. They certainly did not believe the world would end in 2012; they merely calculated a good stopping point for their calendar centuries into the future. However, the humans don't know that. Therefore, we will present *the presumption* that because the Mayan calendar ended on that date, they expected the world to come to an end. How's that for ingenuity? To that we will add other unrelated events to give the appearance that many cultures around the world also predicted the end of the world on or about the same date.

For example, the following unrelated events will be presented as supporting evidence to validate the Mayan's supposed prediction that the world will end on December 21, 2012. The (1) Chinese (I Ching), (2) the Hopi Indians (Prophecy Rock), (3) Nostradamus' vague writings that we can mold into just about any message we want and (4) the Web Bot computer in the United States. Therefore, if the rapture occurs shortly before or shortly after December 21, 2012, as I suspect, we can present the message that multiple cultures from all parts of the world as well as twenty-first century computer technology predicted a big change—it wasn't the Bible. We must continually provide plausible, rational alternatives to Biblical prophecy. We must also cater to their fleshly desires as we blind them to the truth. Let's be sure to give them what their itching ears want to hear.

## ARAB SPRING: AND THE WAR TO COME

As you may have guessed by now, we are currently busy at work laying the foundational framework to launch an attack against Israel that I believe will be one of the final nails in their coffin. I will influence Russia to lead an attack against Israel assisted by ten other countries. This coalition of eleven countries will conduct a coordinated attack against Israel.

If you have read the Bible's book of Ezekiel (chapters 38 and 39) you may already know that this was predicted. Arguably,

Daniel 11 makes reference to this same event; however, I am not 100 percent convinced this last citation is applicable. I state the Daniel 11 citation for the sake of completeness. Suffice it to say, that the Most High has predicted this in writing. If he wants this war, let's give it to him.

The Bible makes the following two predictions: First, it predicts in Ezekiel 39:4-6, 11-12 that this coalition of nations will come against Israel and be wiped out. Secondly, Ezekiel 38:21-23 predicts that soldiers and civilians in the countries they came from will also be wiped out. As always, I have some tricks up my sleeve that the Most High should not be anticipating. To get these countries to work together we had to push some buttons. They have been coasting in status quo for some time. I saw an opening in Tunisia on December 18, 2010, and ran with it. What has come out the other end is what the human media refers to as the "Arab Spring"—a recent wave of revolutions, protests, and demonstrations in the Arab world. The people's collective desire for change finally outweighed their fears of reprisal. It's always fun to capitalize on human tragedy.

The table below is a good summary of the pertinent players. You may have noticed that Tunisia, Bahrain, Jordan, Yemen, Iraq, Kuwait, Oman, Qatar, and the United Arab Emirates (UAE) are not in the table. These countries are part of the Arab Spring but NOT integral players in my plans for the coming onslaught of Israel. I have my reasons, and as always I will not reveal all my thoughts. I will explain in more detail in future communications. Trust me—the eleven countries in the table below are all we will need. *SEE CHART—EZEKIEL 38-39 WAR*

| Countries Identified in the Bible | Scripture Reference | Name of the (11) Modern Day Countries and Type of Government |
|---|---|---|
| 1. Magog | Ezekiel 38-39 | (1) **Russia** (Federation) |
| 2. Persia | Ezekiel 38-39 | (2) **Afghanistan** (Islamic Republic)<br><br>(3) **Pakistan** (Federal Republic)<br><br>(4) **Iran** (Islamic Republic) |
| 3. Cush or Ethiopia | Ezekiel 38-39 | (5) **Somalia** (transitional, parliamentary federal government)<br><br>(6) **Sudan** (power-sharing with an autonomous government in the South)<br><br>(7) **Northern Ethiopia** (Federal Republic) |
| 4. Put | Ezekiel 38-39 | (8) **Libya** (Authoritarian State) |
| 5. Beth Togarmah<br><br>6. Gomer<br><br>7. Meshech<br><br>8. Tubal | Ezekiel 38-39 | (9) **Turkey** (Republic) |
| 9. King of the South | Daniel 11 | (10) **Egypt** (Semi-Presidential Republic) [*democracy*] |
| 10. King of the North | Daniel 11 | (11) **Syria** (Presidential Republic) |

**Chart 3: Countries from the War Predicted in Ezekiel 38-39**

# CHAPTER SIX

# UNEXPLAINED PHENOMENON

*For this reason God sends them a powerful delusion so that they will believe **the lie** and so that all will be condemned who have not believed the truth but have delighted in wickedness. 2 Thessalonians 2:11-12*

## Unexplained Phenomenon:

Most people remember where they were when significant events occurred during their lives. For example, most people remember where they were when they heard the news about President John F. Kennedy's assassination or when they learned of the attacks on September 11, 2001. Ironically, I learned of the attacks on September 11, 2001 while I was sitting in the School Book Depository building (*currently known as the Dallas County Administration building*). I was too focused on the events at hand to absorb the depth of the irony at that time. Now it seems a little surreal and noteworthy.

Having worked in downtown Dallas for years I have heard most every conspiracy theory on the JFK assassination known to man. After a while I found myself tuning out the conspiracy theorists. Frankly, it does not interest me. Similarly, other unexplained events—like the sighting of unidentified flying objects (UFO's) do not intrigue me either. I'm just glad that I've never seen anything that I could not explain. I have no doubt people are seeing *something*. I simply have no idea what UFO's are.

I do remember the first time I saw the X-15 jet aircraft. At first it appeared to be something from outer space. I was shocked to learn that its construction began in 1954. I could hardly believe our military had something like that for many years before it was disclosed to the public. After it was first constructed I wonder how many people would have thought it was from outer space, had they seen it. If I had to guess what UFO's are I would say probably top-secret military aircraft. I simply do not believe little green men from other galaxies are flying spaceships in our atmosphere. Not without credible proof. Similarly I have no idea what cattle mutilations are. No idea, nothing, nada, zilch. I will reserve my conclusions until someone presents me with evidence that I deem to be authenticated, relevant, material, objective, competent and professional. That has not occurred yet.

What **does** interest me is *why* our society is currently being bombarded with messages about UFO's lately. I cannot go to the movies or turn on the television for more than ten minutes without seeing something about UFO's. I do not know why this is occurring, but **there is a reason** for this increase in messaging. As someone who has practiced the professional discipline of investigation for the better part of two decades I know this reason will probably never be known. I'm OK with that. Investigations where forensic analysis is conducted involving cattle mutilations have consistently yielded the presence of 3-Hydroxyanthranilic acid (3HAA). I do not know why 3HAA is present in those samples; however, I know **it's there for a reason**. We will probably never understand these phenomena in our lives. However, I believe it's OK to wonder *why* these occur while simultaneously embracing the notion that we will likely never know.

During any investigation the answer to the question *why* always yields more material information than *what*, *where*, *when*, *how* or *who*. Notwithstanding the improbabilities involved I raise the question of *why* even though I do not believe the answer is forthcoming. I'm OK with that.

# MEMO FROM THE DEVIL:
## PART 6—ALIEN AGENDA

### UNIDENTIFIED FLYING OBJECTS (UFO'S)

We are getting very close to the rapture foretold in John 14:1-3; 1 Corinthians 15:50-58; and 1 Thessalonians 4:13-18. **We DO NOT WANT PEOPLE WHO ARE LEFT BEHIND EVEN THINKING ABOUT THE WORD RAPTURE!** If you do your jobs, this will not even be an eventuality we have to deal with. Once believers are raptured, we will set *"Operation Alien"* into full gear. The people left behind will believe almost anything we proffer as an explanation for the raptured believers. However, to ensure the success of *Operation Alien,* continue indoctrinating the minds of people with the following false extraterrestrial presumptions: (1) aliens from other galaxies actually exist; (2) aliens are flying the UFOs; (3) aliens have been visiting Earth for centuries; and (4) aliens possess advanced intelligence and technology.

Many of you have asked me throughout the ages, *"So what is the lie?"* These questions are referring to the scriptural passage in 2 Thessalonians 2:11-12. As many of you know, I will fabricate a post-rapture cover story that the Most High will even cooperate in.[36] This cover story will be the lie of all lies. A lie that will rival any I have perpetrated over the last several thousand years. For strategic purposes I have historically refused to answer these questions. However, now that we are getting close, I will answer that question with a question.

What is the one event that would create worldwide unity faster than anything? What is the one event that would convince an American soldier to support a Taliban terrorist in less than a second? What is the one event that would unite the world politically, economically, religiously, and culturally in a matter of seconds? Answer: an attack by aliens against planet Earth.

As you well know, alien life forms do not exist in the universe outside of planet Earth. The cover story that aliens from another planet are intelligent and possess advanced space travel is a lie that we have perpetrated for a long time. Now you are about to see why we have laboriously maintained this ruse. When the rapture occurs we will have to be ready to act and act fast. The people who are left behind will be looking for answers and we will hand them a *whopper* on a silver platter. If our recent intelligence analysis is correct approximately 15 percent of the Earth's population of 6.8 billion humans are Christ followers. That is approximately 1.02 billion people who will disappear in the twinkling of an eye. The 5.78 billion people left behind will want to know what just happened. We must be prepared to answer that question.

**The "Lie" is—aliens (*not God*) are responsible for the disappearance of the missing humans, and planet Earth is under attack**. When the Most High begins his sequential series of twenty-one tribulation period judgments (*seven seals, seven trumpets, and seven vials*) humans will attribute many of these judgments as causally connected to the non-existent invading alien armies. This deception will only work if you execute the plans I have disseminated. The absolute most important part of the plan is to have UFOs flying visibly over every corner of the earth within twenty minutes of the rapture. Have all UFO aircraft on "Alert 5" status, twenty-four hours per day. **I want every human left behind to personally witness a UFO hovering above—immediately after the rapture.** I want every television network covering the story, which won't be hard to accomplish.

As most of you already know, we as demonic beings have been posing as *"aliens"* for quite some time. Moreover, we have every major military contractor on the planet in our pocket. Most of these private sector military contractors do not share all they know with their public sector counterparts (*i.e. the military forces around the world*). We the demonic forces have met with military contractors for years. We deceive the private sector contractors and they deceive the military forces who deceive the governments that oversee them. Finally the governments deceive the public. No one knows the whole truth except us. We have shared much of what we know regarding warp drive propulsion systems, aerodynamics, cloaking devices and G-force negation. We have chosen to educate some military contractors much more than others. I may explain that executive decision in more detail in the future. The UFOs that have flown around for years are creations of human private-sector military contractors who think the demons they have been meeting with are little grey men from another planet.

## Propulsion Systems of UFOs

Under Einstein's theory of General Relativity, "gravity" is the result of the curvature of space, caused by mass. Mass causes space to curve and results in the experience of gravity. In other words, the mass of the Earth itself causes space around the planet to curve, producing the experience humans refer to as gravity. The warp drive propulsion systems (*WDPS*) developed for UFOs operate from these principles. The onboard WDPS *expands* space/time behind the UFO and *contracts* space/time in front of the UFO, allowing the UFOs to achieve speeds far exceeding anything the general public understands. The real beauty of the WDPS is the pilots and occupants of UFOs do not experience time dilation or G-Forces.

## Cattle Mutilations by UFOs

The Six-Day War was fought over four decades ago from June 5, 1967 through June 10, 1967. Israel defeated Egypt, Jordan, Iraq, and Syria (*the four strongest Arab countries*) in a mere six days. This scored a deep emotional victory against a coalition of Israel's four biggest enemies. More importantly, the Gentile domination of Jerusalem, which began in A.D. 70 with the Roman invasion by Titus, ended during the Six-Day War in June of 1967. When Israel's army took control of Old Jerusalem it fulfilled a prophetic scripture foretelling this exact event in Luke 21:24.[37] This was the last prophetic scriptural citation that had to be fulfilled before the worldwide spread of the gospel predicted in Matthew 24:14.[38] Due to the difficulty in ascertaining exactly when the Matthew 24:14 prophecy would be fulfilled, I had predetermined that if the Luke 21:24b prophecy was ever fulfilled, we would set into motion our final series of strategies. When I witnessed Luke 21:24b fulfilled in June of 1967, we responded. A few months later in 1967, we commenced quality assurance and quality control tests with the systematic mutilations of cattle, horses, and similar animals with the weapons systems aboard UFO aircraft. Hopefully, no Christ followers will discern that cattle mutilations began in earnest immediately after this fulfilled prophecy. We certainly do not want them to make the connection.

We have been conducting quality control and quality assurance testing on cattle and horses for our laser-guided weapons systems aboard UFOs for years. I am pleased to inform you that the weapons systems are working just fine. The "cattle mutilations," as they are oftentimes referred to by the media, are mere practice sessions for the weapon's true purpose . . . beheading and/or killing humans during the tribulation who will not receive the mark of the beast. Revelation 14:9-11 clearly states that once people receive the mark of the beast their eternal souls are damned and they are ours. It will be a *litmus test* of what has already transpired within their hearts—rejecting Jesus Christ as the Messiah. Some of those who refuse to receive the mark of the beast will have their heads severed from their bodies with the surgical precision of twenty-first century laser technology. Other humans we will target with our weapons which induce apoptosis, which I will explain in more detail below.

From a human perspective, the characteristics of a cattle mutilation typically involve one or more of the following:

- Eyes, ears, genitals and internal organs severed from the body or apparently removed
- Evidence of surgically precise cuts
- Evidence of what appears to be shaving around some of the incisions
- Oblique serrations around some incisions
- Blood from the animals are apparently drained
- No evidence of tracks around the dead carcasses
- No signs of a struggle
- Predators will not go near the dead carcasses
- No missing parts of the dead animals are ever recovered
- Burned grass or burned ground markings near the dead carcasses
- No persons ever caught or adjudicated for causing these deaths

Local authorities who *"investigate"* these events look for and conclude that the deaths are from natural causes. The investigators do not believe the deaths are from natural causes. These conclusions are drawn by authorities in order to prevent panic from the public at large. The authorities know in their hearts that these killings are beyond the scope of scientific understanding; however, they rationalize their findings in light of the consequences which would flow from speaking the truth. It is so easy to deceive the hearts of humans.

You have done a good job rolling out the UFOs with limited exposure. The crop circles, alleged alien abductions, and intermittent UFO sightings have served their purpose of planting the presumption of alien existence into the minds of the humans. Our intelligence analysis currently indicates that approximately 50 percent of humans believe in the existence of aliens from another planet. The other 50 percent will be an easy sale once the Christ followers are gone and the skies are filled with the undeniable existence of *aliens – UFOs flying in plain sight.*

## 3-Hydroxyanthranilic Acid (3HAA)

Some of the blood analysis testing from investigations involving cattle mutilations has revealed the presence of 3-Hydroxyanthranilic acid (3HAA). This concerns me a little because we do not want anyone connecting the presence of 3HAA with what we are actually doing. The presence of 3HAA in cattle mutilations is relevant for two reasons. First, it is one piece of circumstantial evidence that indicates military contractors are utilizing an artificial sclerotization manufacturing process to develop the outer shell coverings for UFOs. Secondly, while it is a metabolite of tryptophan, it is also an integral component of the UFO weapons systems we employ to initiate the process of (*apoptosis*) to achieve programmed cell death (*PCD*) in the targets we shoot.

It all started with observing insects. You can learn a lot by merely watching insects.[39] Some of the insects' shells were hard enough to protect them, yet light enough to allow for flight. Many years ago, I began to consider how we could create a similar process to achieve advanced aircraft. More specifically, I pondered how I could create an artificial manufacturing process for armored exteriors that imitates the cross-linking of the protein chains in the natural sclerotization process.

As you may know, an **arthropod** is an invertebrate animal having an exoskeleton (*external skeleton*), a segmented body, and jointed appendages. Arthropods include the insects, arachnids, crustaceans, and others. A **sclerite** is a hardened portion of arthropod exoskeletons. In arthropods, this hardening is accomplished by the cross-linking of the protein chains in the exocuticle, a process called **sclerotization**. Therefore, the arthropod exoskeleton is divided into numerous sclerites, joined by unsclerotized, membranous regions or sutures. The sclerotization (*or hardening*) of the insect cuticle, for instance, with the consequent formation of a rigid yet light exoskeleton confers both protection and the potential for flight to these arthropods. This is the natural process I copied when I invented the manufacturing process for the exterior shells of UFOs.

**Metabolism** is the set of chemical reactions that occur in living organisms to maintain life. These processes allow organisms to grow and reproduce, maintain their structures, and respond to their environments. Metabolism is usually divided into two categories.

(1) **Catabolism** breaks down organic matter, for example, to harvest energy in cellular respiration, and

(2) **Anabolism** uses energy to construct components of cells such as proteins and nucleic acids.

**Metabolites** are the intermediates and products of metabolism. **Tryptophan** is one of the twenty standard amino acids, as well as an essential amino acid in the human diet. **3-Hydroxyanthranilic acid (3HAA)** is a tryptophan metabolite. Stated another way, 3HAA is an intermediate in the metabolism of tryptophan. It is 3HAA that induces apoptosis in T-cells. I do not believe anyone will discern why 3HAA is often present in the carcasses of mutilated cattle. If you hear humans questioning this, just influence them to believe that someone must have injected the cattle with tryptophan as a tranquilizer; which would explain the presence of 3HAA.

In short, some of our onboard UFO weapons systems artificially induce apoptosis in the targets we shoot. If they work on cattle they will work on humans. We have merely copied another process that occurs in nature. *Apoptosis* or *programmed cell death* is a natural process whereby cells that are no longer needed or are a threat to the organism are destroyed by a tightly regulated cell suicide process. Our weapons induce or trigger that process artificially, which explains why oftentimes internal organs and tissue are missing and blood appears to have been drained from cattle mutilations. I can't wait to use these weapons systems on humans on a larger scale.

## ALIENS AND THE MEDIA

### CABLE TELEVISION

As far as UFOs are concerned, I want cable television shows with increasing frequency to cover UFO-related stories. Per our usual practice, tell no one the actual truth—as deceit will be our vehicle to continue the charade. All these shows should operate with same aforementioned presumptions. More specifically, people should presume that (1) aliens from other galaxies actually exist, (2) aliens are flying the UFOs, (3) aliens have been visiting Earth for eons, and (4) aliens possess advanced intelligence and technology.

### MOVIES WITH ALIENS

Continue influencing movie producers to make movies with extraterrestrials. I also want children's movies with alien themes. We will slowly and methodically continue exposing humans to the false alien presumptions. Before long they will begin to believe these presumptions as fact. Here's a current list of major motion pictures in the last couple of years involving aliens. We have accomplished quite a bit over the last two years. Continue the trend.

| | |
|---|---|
| Aliens in the Attic | 2009 |
| Avatar | 2009 |
| District 9 | 2009 |
| A Genesis Found | 2009 |
| Into the Wild Green Yonder | 2009 |
| Knowing | 2009 |
| Monsters vs. Aliens | 2009 |
| Planet 51 | 2009 |
| Princess of Mars | 2009 |
| Race to Witch Mountain | 2009 |
| The Fourth Kind | 2009 |
| Transformers: Revenge of the Fallen | 2009 |
| Transmorphers: Fall of Man | 2009 |
| Under the Mountain | 2009 |
| Vague | 2009 |
| Megamind | 2010 |
| Monsters | 2010 |
| Predators | 2010 |
| Project Grey — Directors' Cut | 2010 |
| Skyline | 2010 |
| Attack the Block | 2011 |
| Battle: Los Angeles | 2011 |
| Cowboys & Aliens | 2011 |
| Green Lantern | 2011 |
| I Am Number Four | 2011 |
| Mars Needs Moms | 2011 |
| Paul | 2011 |
| Super 8 | 2011 |
| Thor | 2011 |
| Transformers: The Dark of the Moon | 2011 |
| ALIENS | 2012 |
| Apollo 18 | 2012 |

**Chart 4: Movies with Alien Themes**

Finally, should any unforeseen events occur which inhibit our ability to fully execute Operation Alien; we have another strategy that can be employed *with* or *in lieu of* the aforementioned strategy. As you should know, we have placed suicide bombers throughout the world with nuclear weapons of mass destruction (WMD) in various cities. As soon as the rapture occurs, I may give the order to simultaneously detonate these weapons. This would appear as a mere terrorist attack and could explain the disappearance of millions of Christ followers. The humans left behind would presume the missing people were vaporized by a WMD. They would also presume that the brilliant, blinding light they witnessed was the flash of a WMD and not the radiance of Jesus himself. Remember we do not want the humans left behind to realize that Jesus came back to rapture the Christ followers. We must be prepared to offer a plausible counterfeit explanation.

## CHAPTER SEVEN

# WHO IS THE ANTICHRIST?

*"While I was thinking about the horns, there before me was another horn, a little one, which came up among them; and three of the first horns were uprooted before it. This horn had eyes like the eyes of a human being and a mouth that spoke boastfully. Daniel 7:8*

# INTRODUCTION

The word *antichrist* is derived from the original New Testament Greek word pronounced *antichristos,* which means someone who opposes, and/or takes the place of, the true Messiah.[40] The term *"antichrist"* is an often used, yet little understood term. This lack of understanding finds its basis in pure ignorance. Many Christ followers read fictional literature by the truckload, including Christian books. Yet they never pick up the Bible to see what God has to say. Ironically, these same people cannot figure out why they do not understand certain prophetic biblical concepts. I find it fascinating that Christ followers read books *about the Bible* yet don't actually read *the Bible.* The Bible contains more information about the antichrist than any insight human authors can provide. Yet we Christ followers simply don't read the scriptures. I've often wondered if that is why Jesus compared his followers to the dumbest animals on the planet—sheep.

Further, Christ followers often fail to examine the process of original sin to help them gain insight into biblical prophecies. More specifically, the personality the Bible describes as the "man of sin." The antichrist will derive his power, his throne, and his authority from Satan.[41] It is a mistake for the Christ followers to try and understand the antichrist apart from Satan—the person who empowers, enthrones, and authorizes him. For example, this is much like the legal *"principle of agency."* Christ followers mistakenly try and understand the *"agent"* (*antichrist*) separate and apart from the *"principal"* (*Satan*). The antichrist and Satan will be so intertwined he will be noticeable by the similarities he shares with Satan. In short, the antichrist will exemplify behaviors that Satan exemplified as documented in the Bible. For example, one of Satan's behaviors in heaven that made him noticeable was the *abundance of his trade* or his nonstop activities.[42] Therefore, the antichrist might also be noticeable by the abundance of his trade.

The main reason we Christ followers do not understand the antichrist figure is due to reading the Bible less than other extra-biblical sources. We tend to read books about the antichrist; however, we never open the Bible to read what it says about the antichrist. We fail to realize that God would reveal more to us if we merely put the Bible as number one on our priority lists each day.[43] The simple truth is—*If we put God first everything will fall into its proper place.*

I have no idea who the antichrist will be or when he will come. Speaking of Christ's second coming, Matthew 24:36 says, *"But about that day or hour no one knows, not even the angels in heaven, nor the Son, but only the Father."*

If God the Father did not reveal the final timetable to Jesus, you can rest assured he did not tell anyone else. Therefore, since we do not know *the timing* of God's prophesy the forces of good and evil alike must be prepared for his timing at any moment. Due to Satan's intelligence and lack of procrastination, I seriously doubt he has chosen to *sit on his hands* waiting for the rapture to occur before he organizes his forces for the end times. Therefore, he must have to maintain several potential antichrists in every generation.

Assuming Satan has multiple "antichrist" candidates in every generation, no one can ascertain who he will be. Trying to pinpoint exactly who the antichrist will be is impossible. It would be judgmental and sinful to label someone as the antichrist if we guessed wrong. However, the topic *can* be approached by saying, *"Here is what the Bible says and here is what I read in the paper. John Doe **could** potentially be the antichrist."* This is altogether different from what some people do, which is judgmentally stating, *"I know who the antichrist is."* At this point in time the true identity of the antichrist and God's exact timetable are simply not ascertainable. Even Jesus said no man knows the day or the hour of his second coming. However, Jesus never said that we could not ascertain the timetable in general.

# NAMES OF THE ANTICHRIST:

The Bible uses several terms to describe the antichrist. The book of Daniel calls him the *"little horn,"*[44] a *"small horn,"*[45] a *king,*[46] *"the prince who is to come,"*[47] and the *"one who makes desolate."*[48] Other books refer to him doing the *"abomination of desolation."*[49] Jesus referred to him as *"another shall come in his own name."*[50] He is also referred to as the *"man of lawlessness"* and the *"son of destruction."*[51] The New Testament also refers to him as the *liar* and the *antichrist*[52] and *the deceiver,*[53] *the rider of the white horse who conquers,*[54] *the beast,*[55] and the *"man of sin."*[56]

See *Chart—Biblical References to the Names Describing the Antichrist*

| 1. Antichrist, "opposed to/ instead of Christ" | 1 John 2:22 (NIV): Who is the liar? It is the man who denies that Jesus is the Christ. Such a man is **the antichrist**—he denies the Father and the Son. |
|---|---|
| 2. Man of Sin, Son of Perdition, Man of Lawlessness | 2 Thessalonians 2:3 (NIV): Don't let anyone deceive you in any way, for that day will not come until the rebellion occurs and the **man of lawlessness** is revealed, the man doomed to destruction. |
| 3. The Lawless One | 2 Thessalonians 2:8 (NIV): And then the **lawless one** will be revealed, whom the Lord Jesus will overthrow with the breath of his mouth and destroy by the splendor of his coming. |
| 4. The Beast | Revelation 11:7 (NIV): Now when they have finished their testimony, **the beast** that comes up from the Abyss will attack them, and overpower and kill them. |
| 5. The Man of the Earth | Psalm 10:18 (NIV): . . . defending the fatherless and the oppressed, in order that **man, who is of the earth**, may terrify no more. |

| | |
|---|---|
| 6. The Adversary | Psalm 74:8-10 (NIV): They said in their hearts, "We will crush them completely!" They burned every place where God was worshiped in the land. We are given no miraculous signs; no prophets are left, and none of us knows how long this will be. How long will **the adversary** mock you, O God? Will the foe revile your name forever? |
| 7. King, Ruler | Psalm 110:5-6: The Lord is at your right hand; he will crush **kings** on the day of his wrath. He will judge the nations, heaping up the dead and crushing the **rulers** of the whole earth. |
| 8. The Violent Man | Psalm 140:1 (NAS): Rescue me, O LORD, from evil men; Preserve me from **violent men**. |
| 9. King of Babylon | Isaiah 14:4 (NIV): you will take up this taunt against the **king of Babylon**: How the oppressor has come to an end! How his fury has ended! |
| 10. The Spoiler | Isaiah 16:4-5 (NIV): Let My outcasts dwell with you, O Moab; be a shelter to them from the face of **the spoiler**. |
| 11. The Peg (Nail) | Isaiah 22:25: "In that day," declares the LORD Almighty, "**the peg** driven into the firm place will give way; it will be sheared off and will fall, and the load hanging on it will be cut down." The LORD has spoken." |
| 12. The Branch of the Terrible Ones | Isaiah 25:5 (KJV) Thou shalt bring down the noise of strangers, as the heat in a dry place; even the heat with the shadow of a cloud: **the branch of the terrible ones** shall be brought low. |
| 13. The Profane and Wicked Prince of Israel | Ezekiel 21:25-27: (NIV) "'You profane and wicked prince of Israel, whose day has come, whose time of punishment has reached its climax, |
| 14. The Little Horn | Daniel 7:8 (NIV): "While I was thinking about the horns, there before me was **another horn, a little one**, which came up among them; and three of the first horns were uprooted before it. This horn had eyes like the eyes of a human being and a mouth that spoke boastfully. |

| 15. The Prince that Shall Come | Daniel 9:26 (NJKV): And after the sixty-two weeks Messiah shall be cut off, but not for Himself; and the people of the **prince that shall come** shall destroy the city and the sanctuary. |
|---|---|
| 16. The Vile Person | Daniel 11:21 (NKJV): And in his place shall arise a **vile person**, to whom they will not give the honor of royalty; but he shall come in peaceably, and seize the kingdom by intrigue. |
| 17. The Willful King | Daniel 11:36 (NKJV): Then **the king** shall do **according to his own will**: he shall exalt and magnify himself above every god, shall speak blasphemies against the God of gods, and shall prosper till the wrath has been accomplished; for what has been determined shall be done. |
| 18. The Worthless Shepherd | Zechariah 11:16-17 (NKJV): For indeed I will raise up **a shepherd** in the land who will not care for those who are cut off, nor seek the young, nor heal those that are broken, nor feed those that still stand. But he will eat the flesh of the fat and tear their hooves in pieces. "Woe to **the worthless shepherd,** who leaves the flock! A sword shall be against his arm and against his right eye; his arm shall completely wither, and his right eye shall be totally blinded." |
| 19. The Angel of the Abyss (*Bottomless Pit*) Abaddon, Apollyon, Destroyer | Revelation 9:11: (NIV) They had as king over them the **angel of the Abyss**, whose name in Hebrew is **Abaddon** and in Greek is **Apollyon** (that is, **Destroyer**). |

**Chart 5: Biblical References to the Names Describing the Antichrist**

The next table lists possible biblical references (*that I'm less sure about—i.e. **may or may not** refer to the antichrist*). I list these for the sake of completeness.

| 20. Bloody and Deceitful Man | Psalm 5:6: (NIV) You destroy those who tell lies; **bloodthirsty and deceitful men** the LORD abhors. |
|---|---|
| 21. The Wicked Man | Psalm 10:2, 4: (NIV) In his arrogance **the wicked man** hunts down the weak, who are caught in the schemes he devises . . . . In his pride the wicked does not seek him; in all his thoughts there is no room for God. |
| 22. The Mighty Man | Psalm 52:1: (NIV) Why do you boast of evil, you **mighty man**? Why do you boast all day long, you who are a disgrace in the eyes of God? |
| 23. The Enemy | Psalm 55:3: (NIV) . . . at the voice of **the enemy**, at the stares of the wicked; for they bring down suffering upon me and revile me in their anger. |

# HOLY TRINITY V. SATANIC TRINITY:

The doctrine of the "Holy Trinity" is a biblical concept that grows out of the scriptures. The doctrine of the Holy Trinity, however, is not fully and clearly explained. In short, the Holy Trinity is *one God revealed in three persons.* The Father, Son, and Holy Spirit are all equally God, yet they are different persons. Jesus received his authority from the Father.[57] Jesus came in his Father's name.[58] In the gospel of John the Bible states,

> *5:19-23 Jesus gave them this answer: "Very truly I tell you, the Son can do nothing by himself; he can do only what he sees his Father doing, because whatever the Father does the Son also does. For the Father loves the Son and shows him all he does. Yes, and he will show him even greater works than these, so that you will be amazed. For just as the Father raises the dead and gives them life, even so the Son gives life to whom he is pleased to give it. Moreover, the Father judges no one, but has entrusted all judgment to the Son, that all may honor the Son just as they honor the Father. Whoever does not honor the Son does not honor the Father, who sent him.*[59]

It is clear that the persons of the Godhead (*here Father and Son*) are so intertwined they cannot be completely understood apart from each other. They are so much alike, we must study them together to understand them.

Examples of their interrelations include the following. Jesus said to pray to the Father.[60] Jesus is the advocate with the Father.[61] God the Father also gave humans the Holy Spirit.[62] The Holy Spirit never directs attention to himself. The Holy Spirit came at Pentecost in Acts 2:1. Twenty-two verses later, in Acts 2:23 Peter, filled with the Holy Spirit, is preaching about Jesus. The Holy Spirit directs worship and attention to the Son, not himself. Jesus directs us to pray to the Father.

I raised all the aforementioned scripture citations merely to indicate—to understand the antichrist it helps to have a basic understanding of the Holy Trinity. God the Father, God the Son, and God the Holy Spirit form the Holy Trinity. The Holy Trinity is a biblical concept. There are three evil personalities mentioned in prophecy sections of the Bible. These personalities are (1) Satan, (2) the antichrist and (3) the false prophet.[63] In my opinion, the "Satanic trinity" is not a *per se* biblical concept as the Holy Trinity is. However, Satan is the original counterfeiter. Satan passed off his words to Eve as God's words.[64] Satan attempted to pass off his plan to Jesus himself as the Father's plan.[65] Satan is constantly and effectively counterfeiting God's ways. He has also demonstrated a propensity to counterfeit and plagiarize God's original plans.

The Bible describes Satan, the antichrist, and the false prophet as acting in unison. The parallels are obvious. The false prophet's activity mimics that of the Holy Spirit. The false prophet will not direct attention to himself. The false prophet will direct worship to the antichrist,[66] as the Holy Spirit directs worship to Jesus. The false prophet will call fire down from heaven to earth in the presence of men,[67] as the Holy Spirit came down in fire to men.[68] The false prophet will cause all non-believers to receive the mark of the beast,[69] as the Holy Spirit seals believers with a mark for the day of redemption.[70]

In short, the false prophet will mirror his activity to that of the Holy Spirit.

Similarly, Satan's activities often mimic that of God the Father. The entire earth (*except believers*) will worship Satan[71] as the earth worships God the Father.[72] God is the Father of all.[73] Satan is the *"father"* of lies.[74] God's throne is in heaven.[75] Satan desired to raise his throne above the stars of God and wanted to make himself like the Most High.[76] From the beginning Satan wanted to be like God. He still continues counterfeiting the One he most desires to be. *"Imitation"* is the sincerest form of flattery. Satan imitates God because he desires to be like God.

The antichrist will counterfeit himself as the messiah. His coming will be with all power, pretended signs, and wonders.[77] He will take his seat in the temple of God, proclaiming himself to be god.[78] The antichrist will attempt to deceive the world into believing he is the true messiah. He will receive a mortal wound to the head, which will be healed.[79] The antichrist will be wounded with a sword[80] as Jesus was pierced with a spear.[81] God will apparently allow the antichrist to rise from the dead[82] imitating Jesus's resurrection from the dead.

In summation, through the *"Satanic Trinity"* Satan will attempt to counterfeit the true Holy Trinity. Satan will counterfeit himself as God and accept worship from the entire earth. The antichrist will counterfeit himself as the messiah. Finally, the false prophet will imitate the Holy Spirit directing worship of the antichrist.

## CHAPTER EIGHT

# WHEN WILL THE ANTICHRIST COME?

*Let no one in any way deceive you, for it will not come unless the apostasy comes first, and the man of lawlessness is revealed, the son of destruction, 2 Thessalonians 2:3 NAS*

# WHEN WILL THE ANTICHRIST COME?

*"And every spirit that does not confess Jesus is not from God; and this is the spirit of the antichrist, of which you have heard that it is coming, and now it is already in the world."*[83] The spirit of the antichrist must precede the revealing of the man of sin. In the context of this passage John made it very clear. There are two types of people in the world. First, every spirit that confesses Jesus Christ came in the flesh is from God.[84] Every spirit that does not is not from God. It sounds very simple. In a world of gray lines and situational ethics John paints a black and white picture. This spirit of the antichrist must precede the revealing of the man of sin.

In Paul's second letter to the Thessalonians he addressed a body of believers who had been concerned with the end times. Obviously this was in response to Satan having shaken and disturbed the body of believers regarding the *"second coming"* of Jesus.[85] Paul seemed to be saying *"relax, don't be all shook up . . . there are some conditions precedent that must occur before Jesus comes back and they have not happened yet."* Paul then went on to explain three things that must occur before the second coming of Jesus.

First, the apostasy must occur.[86] The Greek word *hē apostasia* literally means a *"falling away."* Satan has successfully indoctrinated unbelievers and some Christ followers alike into believing as he does. Truth is not always the same. Truth is in a constant state of flux. Truth varies depending on the person and depending on the circumstances. What is *"true today"* will not necessarily be *"true tomorrow."* In summary, there is no absolute truth. This prevailing distaste of absolute truth is a *house of cards*. People often fail to notice the antithetical underlying premise. In short, no absolute truth means *there are no absolutes and I'm absolutely sure of it*. Proponents, who say there is no absolute truth, never take notice that **the entire foundation for that belief violates the very statement that**

**rests upon it.** The *sugar* that makes this an easy sale is that— many Christ followers and unbelievers alike want to sit on the thrones of their own lives.

According to recent research, seventy-five to eighty percent of evangelical, fundamental, born-again Christian kids do not believe in absolute truth. Barna Research Group statistics show eighty-one percent of teenagers agree with the following statement; *"When it comes to matters of morals and ethics, truth means different things to different people; no one can be absolutely positive that they know the truth."*[87] Seventy-one percent of teenagers agree with the following statement, *"There is no such thing as 'absolute truth'; two people could define 'truth' in conflicting ways and both could still be correct."*[88] We have an entire generation of born-again Christ followers that are not equipped to differentiate between good and evil because of their fluctuating beliefs on truth. The apostasy will precede the antichrist because most Christians and even more non-believers will not be capable of recognizing him. In short, many Christ followers and unbelievers alike are incapable of recognizing evil when it is staring them in the face, due to their embracing a definition of truth that fluctuates with the circumstances.

Secondly, the man of sin must be revealed.[89] "Paul used a tense for the verb *is revealed* which indicated that this revelation will be a decisive act that will take place at a definite moment in history."[90] This revealing of the man of sin may be coincident with the third precondition.

Thirdly, the restrainer must be removed.[91] There has been much speculation as to what or who the restrainer is. No one knows for sure. I believe the restrainer is the Holy Spirit. Immediately after the church is raptured there will be no Christ followers on the earth. This passage *could* mean that once the church is raptured and taken out of the world, there will be no one left on Earth indwelt by the Holy Spirit. Therefore, there will not be a restraining force to hold back the wave of sin about to hit the planet.

The Bible tells us *"when"* the countdown to the end is imminent. The *"last hour"* of the countdown has been defined: *"Children, it is the last hour; and just as you heard that antichrist is coming, even now many antichrists have appeared; from this we know that it is the last hour."*[92] The real question is why. Why will the number of *"antichrists"* increase at the end? The short answer to that question is . . . . Satan is practicing. Satan is not stupid enough to wait until the rapture actually occurs to possess a world leader for the first time, cross his fingers and hope he can manipulate him into performing his will. Some of his experiments may have involved Saddam Hussein (*Iraq*), Adolf Hitler (*Germany*), Mu-'ammar Gadhafi (*Libya*), Idi Amin Dada (*Uganda*), Ayatollah Khomeini (*Iran*), Josef Stalin (*Russia*), Benito Mussolini (*Italy*), Slobodan Milosevic (*Kosovo*), and Mao Zedong (*China*).

Satan is very intelligent and very determined. Satan is also reading the signs of the end times and coming to his own conclusions about how close the end may be. As the end of the age approaches Satan readies himself to possess the final world ruler, the antichrist.

## WHERE WILL THE ANTICHRIST COME FROM?

The antichrist will come from the *"Roman Empire"* or the present day European-Mediterranean region. Theologians have stated for years that the antichrist will arise from a revived Roman Empire. Theologians often do not explain *why* they believe that. I will give you my opinion on what the scriptures say as plainly and clearly as I can, without sacrificing the comprehensiveness that I deem necessary.

The antichrist will come from the European-Mediterranean area because the Bible specifically makes that prediction three separate times in the book of Daniel. First, the prophecy is referenced in Daniel 2:40-43; secondly, in Daniel 7:17, 23; and thirdly, in Daniel 9:26. We will examine those references as they arise in the book of Daniel.

Nebuchadnezzar, King of Babylon had a dream detailed in the second chapter of Daniel. He dreamt of a statue with four recognizable features. The statue had a head of **gold**. The chest and arms were made of **silver**. The belly and thighs were made of **bronze**. Finally, **iron** made up the legs and the feet consisted of **iron mixed with clay**. (1) Gold, (2) silver, (3) bronze, (4a) iron, then (4b) iron and clay. The value of those metals is juxtaposed against the strength of each metal. For example, as the metals change from top to bottom the *value decreases* as the *strength increases*. Gold is more valuable than iron. However, iron is stronger than gold.

Daniel interprets the dream in Daniel 2:36-43. Daniel informs the king that there will be a succession of four kingdoms, which will rule over all the earth. Daniel tells Nebuchadnezzar he as head of the Babylonian empire is the head of gold.[93] Then Daniel describes the succession of four world empires that will arise before the end. History supports Daniel's interpretation. Nebuchadnezzar's **Babylonian Empire** reigned from 525 B.C. to 457 B.C. The **Medo-Persian Empire** ruled from 457 B.C. to 332 B.C. The **Grecian Empire** led by Alexander the Great ruled from 332 B.C. to 30 B.C. Finally, the **Roman Empire** ruled from 30 B.C. to 476 A.D. That takes us from the head to the ankles. In fact, the accuracy of the book of Daniel is so compelling, some Bible critics believe it was written after-the-fact.

Daniel predicts the fourth kingdom will shatter, break, and crush all things.[94] An angel interprets the meaning of this fourth part (*iron*) of the statue. The angel tells Daniel the fourth part of the statue in Nebuchadnezzar's dream is the same thing as the *fourth beast* in Daniel's dream.[95] This fourth kingdom, of the antichrist, will conquer the entire world. We know from history that the fourth kingdom was the Roman Empire, which was finally conquered in 476 A.D. In short, the Bible predicted that the antichrist and his fourth kingdom

(*Roman Empire*) will conquer the entire world. That has not happened to date; however, it will happen as we race towards the New World Order.

Daniel had a dream and visions about four beasts detailed in chapter 7. The first beast was a **lion** with eagle's wings, standing as a man, given a man's heart. The second beast was a **bear** raised up on one side, with three ribs in its mouth. The third was a **leopard** with four wings of a fowl, it had four heads. The **fourth beast** had ten horns, bronze claws. It was described as dreadful, terrifying, strong, and it had large iron teeth which devoured. It crushed, trampled, and it was different from all the others before it. History also supports Daniel's dream. The first beast is the Babylonian Empire. The two animals that symbolized the Babylonian Empire were the eagle and the lion. The second beast is the Medo-Persian Empire. The Persians were stronger than the Medes hence the second beast is raised up on one side.[96] The Medo-Persians conquered three countries, Babylon, Egypt, and Lydia. This is likely symbolized by the three ribs in the beast's mouth. The third beast is the Greek Empire. After Alexander the Great's death, his empire was divided up into four smaller empires. This is likely symbolized by the four heads. Finally, the fourth beast is the Roman Empire.

The meaning of the fourth beast is explained by the angel. The angel tells Daniel the fourth beast is a king[97] and a kingdom.[98] This is the antichrist and his future kingdom, the Roman Empire. What the angel is essentially saying is the bottom part of the statue (*feet of iron mixed with clay*) in Nebuchadnezzar's dream[99] is the same thing as the fourth beast in Daniel's dream. The current European Union consists of approximately twenty-seven countries. Europe currently consists of different languages, different cultures, and different races of people. This melting pot of differences likens itself to mixing iron and clay.[100] You can mix it together but it won't stick.

Finally, the Bible identifies the ethnicity of the antichrist. The antichrist, or the *"prince who shall come,"* will be from the same race of people that destroys the temple in Jerusalem.[101] From that point forward all anyone had to do was sit back and see what race of people destroyed the temple. In 70 A.D. Roman emperor Titus marched into Jerusalem and destroyed the temple. Many of the precious artifacts inside the temple burned and melted into the mortar between the stones of the temple. He and his troops literally tore the temple apart stone by stone, to recover the melted gold and silver. This literally fulfilled Jesus's prophecy, when he prophesied *"not one stone here shall be left upon another."*[102]

In summation, the antichrist will arise from the geographical area of the world we know as the modern day European-Mediterranean region. We know this is where he will arise because the Bible states in three different places that he and his kingdom will conquer the entire world. The antichrist's kingdom is described as the fourth part of the statue in Nebuchadnezzar's dream (*feet of iron mixed with clay*). It is also described as the fourth beast in Daniel's dream. Finally, the antichrist's people are defined as those who will one day destroy the temple. History has shown us a succession of kingdoms mirroring exactly (1) the succession of kingdoms in Nebuchadnezzar's dream, and (2) the succession of kingdoms in Daniel's dream and visions. History has shown us the fourth kingdom was the Roman Empire. We have literally witnessed the reviving of that empire since the Treaty of Rome was signed in 1957. Finally, history has shown us that the Romans were the people who destroyed the temple in Jerusalem.

For the Christ followers who actually read and understand prophecy, most are watching the European Union (EU) because they presume the antichrist's kingdom will arise from the EU's governmental structure (*public sector*). However, the final kingdom could arise from the other side (*private sector*).

# CHAPTER NINE

## COMPARING BIBLE VERSES TO NEWS ARTICLES

*Jesus answered: "Watch out that no one deceives you." Matthew 24:4 NIV*

# SILVIO BERLUSCONI: NEWS ARTICLES

As previously stated, Satan must have several antichrist candidates in every generation. While no one knows who the antichrist will be, it is oftentimes interesting to read your Bible in one hand with the newspaper in the other. One example of a leader who appears to match some of the Bible's descriptions is Silvio Berlusconi, the current Italian Prime Minister.

> *Mr. Berlusconi has succeeded in imposing himself on the international stage. Italy is the world's fifth largest economic power, the third contributor to UN peace missions, the third contributor to the European Union and the sixth to the United Nations, he told Panorama. Could he try harder? Not really. Mr. Berlusconi is already prone to hyperactivity and taking on interim responsibility for the foreign ministry was probably unwise. He should slow down and take time off for reflection.*[103]

From March 1, 2002 to March 6, 2003, Silvio Berlusconi had 189 international appointments.[104] That is a busy international agenda for a relatively small country. Berlusconi is probably just another run-of-the mill world leader. However, his international activity is extremely high and one of his trademarks.

1.  **Described as "little" compared to other surrounding leaders (little horn) (Daniel 7:8)**

*"(A) Carefully controlled image is vital to Berlusconi's sense of himself. His lighting cameraman goes ahead to meetings; the short stature is carefully angled up (i.e. camera angled to make him look taller) . . . and a box to stand on put behind the podium."*[105]

2.  **Mouth speaking great things (Daniel 7:8)**
    a.  **Mouth that spoke great things (Daniel 7:20)**

### b. The Beast was given a mouth uttering haughty and blasphemous words (Revelation 13:5)

Mr. Berlusconi made the following statement to CNN in 2001, *"Because of my personal history, my professional skills and my business achievements, I am a man nobody can expect to compare himself with."*[106]

### 3. Have a fierce countenance (bold countenance, stern) (Daniel 8:23)

This prophecy *does not* mean the antichrist cannot smile. What it *does* mean is that one of his identifying physical features will be a stern or fierce countenance. The reader can examine his photographs and come to their own conclusions.

### 4. He will be different than the kings before him (Daniel 7:24)

*There has never been a phenomenon in any western democracy to compare to Berlusconi, but there will surely be more to come. The novelist Umberto Eco said Berlusconi was the first to understand the collapse of traditional ideology in Italy and its replacement by mass media. And this was Berlusconi's 'masterpiece of synthesis', his unique contribution to the global media culture: the combination of business, TV, marketing and politics. He is a prototype of what may already be incubating: a new race of media monopolist politicians. This is partly what lay behind the jitters at his arrival: if you invented a cyber-candidate for the US that combined Rupert Murdoch, Ross Perot, Michael Bloomberg and Ronald Reagan, you still wouldn't have his equivalent. He is the 29th richest man in the world, worth $12 billion; he has a near monopoly of commercial TV in Italy and now, as prime minister, the patronage of state TV; he owns the dominating chunk of the Italian print and publishing media; his film production company is Italy's biggest. And he refuses to part with any of it.*[107]

## 5. His coming will be with all power, pretended signs, wonders, and the activity of Satan (2 Thessalonians 2:9)

Berlusconi has made statements that would be political suicide for most politicians. He has claimed to perform miracles. *"(He) was quoted as saying that he had once told a young man confined to a wheelchair that he should get up and walk—which the disabled person actually did a few days later. The Pope is not expected to recognize the miracle."*[108] The truly miraculous component of his claims is the fact that his claims are given such little media attention. If a multi-billionaire anywhere else in the world began to *"perform miracles"* there would be some interesting media coverage. The same could be said of a world leader anywhere else. The same could be said of a media-magnate anywhere else. Berlusconi is a multi-billionaire, a world leader, and a media-magnate, and not many people seem to notice his outrageous comments. Now that is miraculous.

## 6. He shall think to change the times and law. (Daniel 7:25)

One of Berlusconi's first acts as prime minister was to change some of the laws involving white-collar crime. *"He has passed laws that serve his own interests, including one that decriminalized false accounting—which took care of three major charges against him. Legislation is being drawn up to weaken the power of magistrates . . . ."*[109] In October of 2001,

> *Berlusconi's government approved a law making it more difficult for Italian magistrates to investigate suspicious cross-border financial flows. Another bill passed last month will partly decriminalize false accounting, shorten the statute of limitations on such cases, and sharply reduce the penalties for those found guilty. Berlusconi backers in Parliament say the new law restricting the use of cross-border evidence will protect individuals from prosecution based on false documents. But it's no secret that the laws will also directly benefit Berlusconi—*

*by derailing pending lawsuits against him for tax fraud, false accounting, and bribery. Indeed, portions of the controversial legislation were drafted by his former defense lawyer.*[110]

## 7. He will be "the lawless one." (2 Thessalonians 2:8)

Silvio Berlusconi has faced multiple criminal prosecutions. Below is a criminal history chart[111] with some of the criminal charges brought against him. *See Chart—Berlusconi's Criminal History*[112]

| Status of trial | | Allegation |
|---|---|---|
| Dropped trials | Time limits extinct crimes | • LodoMondadori: bribery of judges (statute of limitation acquittal)<br>• All Iberian 1:23 bilions Liras bribe to Bettino Craxi via an offshore bank account code-named All Iberian (first court sentence: 2 years 4 months jail; appeal: acquitted since the statute of limitations expired before the appeal)<br>• Lentini affair: false accounting (not guilty because of changes in the false accounting law) |
| | Amnesty extinct crimes | • Propaganda Due (P2) masonic lodge trial: false testimony (guilty but amnesty applied)<br>• Macherio estates: false accounting (amnesty applied following the 1992 fiscal remission law) |

| Acquittals | Acquittal for variation of the Law | • All Iberian 2: false accounting (acquittal following the new law on the false accounting passed by the Berlusconi government) <br> • Sme-Ariosto 2: false accounting (acquittal following the new law on the false accounting passed by the Berlusconi government) |
|---|---|---|
| | Other acquittals | • Sme-Ariosto 1: charge for the sale by IRI, bribes to judges (first instance court sentence) <br> • Bribery of the Guardia di Finanza (first sentence: 2 years 9 months jail; appeal: statute of limitations for 3 charges, acquittal for the fourth (not proven) <br> • Medusa Cinema company: false accounting (acquitted since too rich for being aware of such small amounts) <br> • Sme-Ariosto 1: bribes to the judge Renato Squillante <br> • Macherio estates: embezzlement, tax evasion, another false accounting (the statute of limitations expired before the first court verdict for one charge; and before the appeal court for the second one) <br> • Television rights: false accounting, tax evasion, embezzlement |

| Archived trials | Archiving for variation of the Law | • Fininvest financial statement: false accounting and embezzlement (archived thanks to the new law on the false accounting passed by the Berlusconi government) <br> • Fininvest consolidated financial statements: false accounting (archived thanks to the new law on the false accounting passed by the Berlusconi government) |
| --- | --- | --- |
| | Other archived trials | • Agreement on the division of publicity between RAI and Fininvest televisions <br> • Traffic of drugs <br> • Tax bribery on the Pay-tv <br> • Collusion into the 1992-1993 slaughters <br> • Mafia collusion, together with Marcello Dell'Utri, money laundering |
| Ongoing trials | | • Bribe to the lawyer David Mills: corruption to influence a judiciary sentence <br> • Corruption of senators of the Romano Prodi government camp (procedure transferred from Naples to Rome) <br> • Paying an underage girl (Karima el-Mahroug) for sex and abuse of office relating to her release from detention |

**Chart 6: Silvio Berlusconi's Criminal History**

8. but every spirit that does not acknowledge Jesus is not from God. This is the spirit of the antichrist, which you have heard is coming and even now is already in the world. (1 John 4:3)

   He will not acknowledge the coming of Jesus in the flesh (2 John 1:7)

Italy is a country filled with people who are *Catholic*. I have failed to locate any documentation that he has ever publicly confessed Jesus as Lord. Nor have I been able to locate information that he has ever acknowledged that Jesus Christ came into this world as a man. The fact that there was once a man named Jesus Christ who died approximately two thousand years ago is a fact of history. Arguably, Berlusconi could *disqualify* himself as a potential antichrist candidate if he would merely admit that Jesus Christ came in the flesh. Finally, most Christ followers fail to see the connection between 1 John 4:3 and 2 John 1:7.

9. It (antichrist) magnified itself, even up to the Prince of Host (Daniel 8:11)
   a. He will magnify himself in his own mind (Daniel 8:25)
   b. He will magnify himself above every god (Daniel 11:36)
   c. He will magnify himself above all (Daniel 11:37)

Berlusconi once commented: *"There is no one on the international scene who can presume to measure up to me. My greatness is unquestionable, my humanity, my history—others can only dream of such."*[113] He has also been quoted as saying, *"There is no one on the world stage who can compete with me"*.[114] *"He has a huge ego, and has often said that no man can compare himself to him, because of all that he has accomplished."*[115]

10. **His power shall be great (Daniel 8:24)**

   **Authority was given to it over every tribe and people and tongue and nation, and all who dwell on the Earth will worship it (Non-Christians) (Revelation13:7)**

   *He is a two-time Prime Minister of his country. He is also the richest man in his country, whose empire includes one of the most valuable sports franchises in the world, the largest private TV network company in Europe, a publishing conglomerate, a bank, insurance companies, and department stores. He is worth over $10 billion US dollars.*[116]

11. **He will destroy to an extraordinary degree (Daniel 8:24)**
   a. **Destroy many without warning (Daniel 8:25)**
   b. **Go forth with great fury to exterminate and utterly destroy (Daniel 11:44)**

   *"He can be an irate person,"* says James Walston, a university professor of political science. *"If he loses his cool at the wrong time, it could cause some sort of crisis. Will he survive a five-year term? I wouldn't bet on it."*[117] Would a man with this kind of power actually think in terms of a global revolution? *"Sunk deep in a sofa in his palace, Berlusconi grins and explains why Europe has nothing to fear from his coming revolution. We are preparing a Copernican Revolution to refound the state."*[118]

12. **He will succeed in what he does (Daniel 8:24)**
   a. **He will do according to his will (Daniel 8:36)**
   b. **He will prosper until the indignation is accomplished (Daniel 11:36)**

   Berlusconi is one of the most successful people in the world. *"He is his country's wealthiest man, and ranked on Forbes list as the wealthiest politician in the world, with an estimated net worth of $12.8 billion."*[119]

### 13. He will make deceit prosper by his cunning (Daniel 8:25)

*He refers to himself as a man of 'all the people,' from blue-collar workers and entrepreneurs to farmers, and he has <u>often been accused of taking on different personas</u> . . . To craftsmen, he tells the story of how he laid out the carpet in his first office. To farmers, he tells them how he helped farm the fields of his parents. To businessmen, he shows them his Ferraris and says, 'I am one of you.'"*[120] *"He is described, almost affectionately, by friends and foes alike, as a championship-class liar."*[121] *"Opponents have compared him to Zelig, the Woody Allen movie character whose appearance blends in with every person he talks to."*[122] *"Antonio Di Pietro, an MP who investigated Mr Berlusconi as one of Milan's anti-corruption prosecutors, said the prime minister deserved a Nobel prize for lying. 'Our country is ridiculed abroad thanks to Silvio Berlusconi. That, unfortunately, is the bitter truth,' he said.*[123]

### 14. Make a covenant with the many for seven years (Daniel 9:27)

Berlusconi fired his foreign minister in January of 2002 due to philosophical differences. *"Prime Minister has named himself foreign minister following the resignation of his former foreign minister. BBC correspondent David Willey says it is unclear how the prime minister will manage to do both jobs.*[124] Immediately after getting rid of his foreign minister, Berlusconi began international peace negotiations in the Middle East. The Prime Minister voiced his country's support . . . to bring lasting peace to the Middle East. *"I will carry Prince Abdullah's peace message to the European Council."*[125]

### 15. He will magnify those who honor him (Daniel 11:39)
  a. Make them rulers over many (Daniel 11:39)
  b. Divide the land for a price (Daniel 11:39)

Once the antichrist assumes power, he will divide property and sell it for a price. The antichrist *may* have a background in real estate. Berlusconi made his first millions in the real estate industry. *"I've been a property developer, it's what I'm best at. Soon I'll be able to develop the whole country."*[126]

**16. The whole earth followed him with wonder (Revelation 13:3)**
   **a. People will say, "Who is like the beast? Who can fight against him? (Revelation 13:4)**
   **b. Whole world will marvel to behold the Beast (Revelation 17:8)**

Silvio Berlusconi has referred to himself as the *"Messiah." "Mr Berlusconi has a tendency to compare himself to the Messiah. No one is quite sure whether he is joking."*[127] *"Berlusconi became the target of satirical jokes when he called himself 'the anointed of the Lord'."*[128]

**17. Rider of white horse, with a bow, and a crown, went out to conquer . . . its rider was named Death (Revelation 6:2)**

The reference to the rider of the white horse in Revelation 6:2 may be a reference to the antichrist. The white horse may signify a rider who will conquer with peace. This could be further explained by the symbolic bow and no arrows. In the early stages, the antichrist may conquer and assume power through peace. Berlusconi was nominated for the 2003 Nobel Peace Prize, awarded in October each year. *"He has been nominated for the (2003) Nobel Peace Prize for, his successful mediation in the siege of Bethlehem's Church of the Nativity last May and his efforts to promote a rapprochement between NATO and Russia were all signs of his statesman-like service to the cause of peace . . . These were three strong international initiatives . . . For the first time Italy has assumed the role of a protagonist on the international stage and it is all the merit of Mr. Berlusconi."*[129]

## OBSERVATIONS:

Jesus told the Pharisees, *"For the mouth speaks out of that which fills the heart."*[130] If you ever desire to know what is in a person's heart, just listen to what comes out of his or her mouth. You can examine the hearts of *potential antichrists* by the words that come from their mouths. The antichrist will one day present himself as the savior of the world. The antichrist will declare himself to be God and demand that the entire earth worship him and receive his mark of the beast.[131]

No one knows who the antichrist will be. Satan must have several candidates in each generation in the event that any of them were to die suddenly. However, Berlusconi is merely one possibility. He fits some of the profile as the wealthiest politician in the world, and one of the shortest of the European leaders. He is a world leader who runs an entire country and has claimed to perform miracles. Arguably he magnifies himself in his own mind as evidenced by his repeated statements about himself. He is a unique politician. He has thrust himself into the Middle East peace process. He sponsored Saudi Crown Prince Abdullah's peace plan by bringing it to the European Union. He referred to himself as *"the Messiah"* and as *"the anointed of the Lord."* In earthly realms he is very powerful and influential. He has a track record of changing the laws. He was nominated for the 2003 Nobel Peace Prize. He has been described as a *"world class liar."* He has a criminal history. The most interesting thing about Mr. Berlusconi is that most people in the Western hemisphere have never heard of him. Silvio Berlusconi is just one potential candidate in this generation. He appears to meet some of the biblical characteristics of the future antichrist. Now would be a good time for Christ followers to read their newspaper in one hand with their Bible in the other.

# CHAPTER TEN

## BIBLICAL REFERENCES TO THE ANTICHRIST

*Therefore rejoice, you heavens and you who dwell in them! But woe to the earth and the sea, because the devil has gone down to you! He is filled with fury, because he knows that his time is short." Revelation 12:12*

# Bible Verses Regarding the Antichrist

1) Described as "little" compared to other surrounding leaders (little horn) (Daniel 7:8)

2) Had "eyes like the eyes of a man" (Daniel 7:8)

3) Had eyes (Daniel 7:20)

4) Mouth that spoke boastfully (Daniel 7:8)

5) Mouth that spoke boastfully (Daniel 7:20)

6) And there was given unto him a mouth speaking great things and blasphemies (Revelation 13:5)

7) Have a stern face (*fierce countenance, bold countenance, insolent*) (Daniel 8:23)

8) Looked more imposing than the others (Daniel 7:20)

9) He will be different than the kings before him (Daniel 7:24)

10) Arises among ten kings. (Daniel 7:8, 20, 24)

11) *Daniel 8:23-25: is likely a dual reference to Antiochus IV Epiphanes and the Antichrist*

12) His coming will be with counterfeit miracles, signs and wonders, and the work of Satan (2 Thessalonians 2:9)

13) Three kings fall (Daniel 7:20)

    a) He will subdue three kings (Daniel 7:24)

14) Waging war against the saints (Christians), and defeating them. (Daniel 7:21)

15) Oppress the saints of the Most High (Daniel 7:25)

16) Saints will be given into his hand for three and one-half years (Daniel 7:25)

17) *He will destroy the mighty men and holy people (Daniel 8:24) [likely a dual reference, see supra]*

18) He was given power to make war on the saints and to conquer them (Revelation 13:7)

19) He will speak words against the Most High (God) (Daniel 7:25)

20) He will say unheard of things against God (Daniel 11:36)

21) He opened its mouth to blaspheme God, slander his name, his dwelling place, and those who live in heaven (Revelation 13:6)

22) He will try to change the set times and the laws. (Daniel 7:25)

23) He will not acknowledge the coming of Jesus Christ in the flesh (2 John 1:7)

24) Magnify himself

    a)   He will consider himself superior (Daniel 8:25)

    b)   He will exalt and magnify himself above every god (Daniel 11:36)

    c)   He will exalt himself above them all (Daniel 11:37)

25) Master of intrigue (Daniel 8:23)

26) He will become very strong (Daniel 8:24)

    a)   Authority was given to it over every tribe, people, language and nation, and all inhabitants of the Earth will worship the beast (Non-Christians) (Revelation 13:7-8)

27) He will cause astounding devastation (Daniel 8:24)

a) Destroy many when they feel secure (Daniel 8:25)

b) Set out in great rage to destroy and annihilate many (Daniel 11:44)

28) Pitch his royal tents between the seas and beautiful holy mountain (Daniel 11:45)

29) Rider of white horse, with a bow, and a crown, went out to conquer (Revelation 6:2)

30) He will succeed in whatever he does (Daniel 8:24)

a) He will be successful until the time of wrath is completed (Daniel 11:36)

b) Will do as he pleases (Daniel 11:36)

31) He will destroy mighty men (Daniel 8:24)

32) He will cause deceit to prosper (Daniel 8:25)

33) Confirm a covenant with the many for 7 years (Daniel 9:27)

a) First 3 ½ years re-institute sacrifices in temple (Daniel 9:27)

34) Show no regard for the gods of his fathers (Daniel 11:37)

35) Opposes and exalts himself above everything that is called god or worshipped (2 Thessalonians 2:4)

36) Denies the Father and that Jesus is the Christ (1 John 2:22)

37) The spirit of the antichrist does not acknowledge Jesus (1 John 4:3)

38) He will not acknowledge the coming of Jesus Christ in the flesh (2 John 1:7)

39) Show no regard for the one desired by women (Daniel 11:37)

40) He will honor a "god of fortresses" (Daniel 11:38)

41) He will honor a god his forefathers did not know (Daniel 11:38)

42) He will honor with gold, silver, precious stones, costly gifts (Daniel 11:38)

43) He will greatly honor those who acknowledge him (Daniel 11:39)

44) Make them rulers over many people (Daniel 11:39)

45) Distribute the land at a price (Daniel 11:39)

46) He will be attacked by the king of the south (*Egypt*) and king of the north (*Syria*) (Daniel 11:40)

47) Respond by invading the Beautiful Land (*Israel*) (Daniel 11:41)

48) Many countries will fall, but some will be delivered out of his hand (Daniel 11:41)

49) Extend his power over many countries, and Egypt (Daniel 11:42)

50) Abomination that causes desolation standing in the holy place (Matthew 24:15; Daniel 9:27; 11:31; Mark 13:14)

51) Takes his seat in the temple of God, proclaiming himself to be God (2 Thessalonians 2:4)

52) His "image" (*statue?*) will speak, and cause those who do not worship the image to be slain. (Revelation 13:14-15)

53) He will come in his own name and be accepted by those who reject Jesus (John 5:43)

54) Receives a fatal wound to the head, which will heal (Revelation 13:3)

55) Fatal wound will be healed (Revelation 13:12)

56) Wound will be from a sword (Revelation 13:14)

57) Once was, now is not, and will come up out of the abyss (Revelation 17:8)

58) "May the sword strike his arm and his right eye! May his arm be completely withered, his right eye totally blinded!" (Zechariah 11:17)

59) The whole Earth is astonished and followed him (Revelation 13:3)

60) People will say "Who is like the beast? Who can make war against him? (Revelation 13:4)

61) Whole world will be astonished when they see the beast (Revelation 17:8)

62) Exercised authority for 42 months (Revelation 13:5)

63) Mark of the Beast (666) is the name of the beast or the number of his name (Revelation 13:18)

   (a) The name of the Beast will somehow be associated with the number 666 (Revelation 13:18)

(b) Some manuscripts read 616

64) No one will be able to buy or sell without his mark after the midpoint of the tribulation (Revelation 13:17)

65) Gather forces to war against God and his army (Revelation 19:19)

66) Ultimately he will be slain, body destroyed, given over to fire. (Daniel 7:11)

67) His power will be taken away and destroyed forever (Daniel 7:26)

68) He will be destroyed, but not by human power (Daniel 8:25)

69) Jesus will overthrow him with the breath of his mouth (2 Thessalonians 2:8)

70) He will be destroyed by the splendor of Jesus's coming (2 Thessalonians 2:8)

71) Thrown alive into the fiery lake of burning sulfur (Revelation 19:20)

# MEMO FROM THE DEVIL: PART 7—THE COMING PRINCE

Do you remember the Jewish Holocaust when we killed over six million Jews? Not to mention an additional eleven million civilians. Stop for a minute and remember the concentration camps. As you should recall, we guided the Nazi guards to recite a series of instructions to all the Jewish prisoners destined for death. In a very polite tone each guard would give the following speech.

> *I know each of you is anxious to get cleaned up and have a hot meal. In order to facilitate an orderly process we will ask you to disrobe for your shower and form a line in single file. Please tie your shoe laces together to enable you to find your shoes more easily when you are through with your shower. As you can see there are several hooks for you to hang your clothes on. Please ensure that all your clothes are placed on one hook. Please place your shoes on the floor immediately beneath the hook on which your clothes are hanging. If you will notice each hook has a number sign above it. Please remember your number so you can find your clothes and shoes as soon as you are through with your shower. The guards are now handing you a bar of soap. Please hang onto this after you have completed your shower so you can use it throughout the week.*

Does that bring back any memories? The bars of soap and the number signs above the hooks were props. The smiling faces and congenial tones of the guards were a ruse. The carts with fresh clean towels which were folded and neatly stacked were pure theater. Our goal was to get them into the gas chambers without a struggle. We used this very simple strategy to voluntarily walk millions of Jews right into the gas chambers. Not one of them resisted. It worked because our counterfeit explanation was appealing, attractive, encouraging, caring, intelligent, and plausible. They never saw it coming. Neither will they sense danger with the coming prince.

As you know, I have orchestrated a group of potential antichrist candidates in every generation since 1948. Every one of these men has the gift of subtlety. When it comes time for me to make a choice, I will walk him from the shadows of obscurity onto the bright lights of the world stage the exact same way. His foreign and domestic policies will be appealing. His answers for the economic collapse and resulting inflation will be attractive. His plans for world peace will garner unparalleled encouragement from the masses. His thoughtful, intelligent remarks will display a matchless plausibility. All of this is designed to accomplish the exact same goal from the concentration camps 60 years ago. Wipe the Israelites off the map.

Once we eradicate the Jews from existence, the Most High will not be able to keep his promises. In short he will become that which he abhors—a liar. Once that goal is accomplished he will no longer possess the moral authority to go forward with his plans in attempting to cast us in the lake of fire. Moral authority is a condition precedent to righteous judgment. Our goal is not to just make him a liar—but to divest him of the very character that makes him what he is.

Many antichrists have already arisen. From this fact you can ascertain that we are in the last hour and the final prince is coming. We certainly have had fun with some of the world leaders portrayed as maniacal dictators. We have piled up the bodies with many of these monsters. If you added together all the vicious and predatory characteristics of the murderous world leaders over time, it would not approach what I am going to do with the little horn. Once I move him into position it will take about three and a half years to lull the world into a place where I want them, before I bare the bronze claws and iron teeth of terror.

The hidden beauty of our deception resides within the private sector. Very few people have noticed that the controls of our network will reside within the private sector not the governmental sector. I will explain more about the network below. As we utilize the financial systems to dismantle governmental infrastructures around the world we will simultaneously piece together the various components of the network. The beast's rise to power will begin shortly and will correspond with the slow, methodical assembly of the network. They will never see him coming.

# CHAPTER ELEVEN

## THE COMMON DENOMINATOR FOR THE MARK OF THE BEAST (EPC/RFID)

*And he causeth all, both small and great, rich and poor, free and bond, to receive a mark **in** their right hand, or **in** their foreheads:And that no man might buy or sell, save he that had the mark, or the name of the beast, or the number of his name. Revelation 13:16-17KJV*

# ELECTRONIC PRODUCT CODE/RADIO FREQUENCY IDENTIFICATION

To better understand where the world is going we must appreciate the future in the context of technological developments and movements including; (1) the Sunrise Date, (2) the global consolidation of barcode governing councils; (3) the European Union's Galileo satellite system; (4) the five major entities who have legislated, financed, designed, implemented, and currently control these developments; (5) Radio Frequency Identification [RFID]; (6) RFID applications; and (7) biometrics [132]and transponders.

American and European technological marking systems (*barcodes*) appear to be unrelated at first glance; however, they are related. The common denominator that will bind these elements together is the Electronic Product Code (EPC) and RFID.

# WHY THE EUROPEAN UNION WANTS TO CONTROL THE INTERNET

## *THE INTERNET: DIVERGENT VISIONS AND CONTROL*

The United States and the European Union (EU) have differing views of the Internet. The United States envisions the Internet as a worldwide web of **data**, which it currently is. The United States controls the Internet and has begun a program to consolidate access to its existing databases.

Control of the Internet can be summarized in five primary areas; (1) who operates the database of generic names; (2) who appoints the operators for two-letter country code suffixes; (3) who decides Internet Protocol number allocation; (4) who controls the root servers; and (5) who establishes the technical standards.[133] The EU desires to participate in control of the Internet. In 2005, the United States responded to the EU's pressure by issuing a statement declining the invitation to share that control. [134]

Europe, on the other hand, envisions a worldwide web of **all things**. The EU has developed a ground system called European Geostationary Navigation Overlay Service (EGNOS) and a satellite system called Galileo, which together can monitor EPC-marked items via RFID technology.

### GALILEO AND THE RACE TO CONTROL INFORMATION

For obvious reasons, the United States is concerned about the EU's new Galileo satellite system. In a letter dated December 3, 2001, former Deputy Secretary of Defense Paul Wolfowitz expressed security concerns over Galileo's (1) signal development, (2) the civil forum the EU has chosen to develop Galileo, and (3) whether the EU intends to use Galileo for military purposes.[135] EU officials not only acknowledge the United States' concerns, but characterize Galileo as the future world standard. Francois Lamoureux, Director General for Energy and Transport of the European Commission, stated, "[a]nd then we have an agreement with the US. They didn't like Galileo for a long time, but we made peace and now there is an agreement which allows interoperability and will make Galileo the world standard."[136]

Preparations have already begun for a world aligned with the EU's vision of a worldwide web of all things. In 2002, the United States began a program to consolidate access to its existing databases. John Poindexter stated, "Total Information Awareness—a prototype system—is our answer. We must be able to detect, classify, identify, and track terrorists so that we may understand their plans and act to prevent them from being executed. To protect our rights, we must ensure that our systems track the terrorists, and those that mean us harm."[137]

The new world order, as the EU envisions it, will be one of true interconnectivity and devoid of anonymity. Ann Cavoukian, Information and Privacy Commissioner in Toronto, Canada, stated, "John Poindexter, head of the Pentagon's Office of Information Awareness (OIA), is developing a vast surveillance database to track terror suspects . . . (TIA) system will, 'break down the stovepipes' that separate commercial and government databases, allowing OIA access to citizens' credit card purchases, travel itineraries, telephone calling records, email, medical histories and financial information. TIA will give the United States government the power to generate a comprehensive data profile on any U.S. citizen."[138]

The technology now exists to have everything on Earth numbered, identified, catalogued, and tracked. "RFID employs a numbering scheme called EPC . . . which can provide a unique ID for any physical object in the world. The EPC is intended to replace the UPC bar code used on products today. Unlike the bar code, however, the EPC goes beyond identifying product categories—it actually assigns a unique number to every single item that rolls off a manufacturing line. For example, each pack of cigarettes, individual can of soda, light bulb, or package of razor blades produced would be uniquely identifiable through its own EPC number."[139]

Some have speculated that EU's vision of an Internet-connected world or a worldwide web of all things is a certainty, not a possibility. Computer databases and systems all over the world are being linked together with increasingly regularity. RFID tags and the accompanying technologies are spreading even faster. Dirk Heyman, global head of life science and consumer product industries at Sun Microsystems, Inc. stated, "In the near future every single object will be connected to the Internet through a wireless address and unique identifier".[140]

# THE ELECTRONIC PRODUCT CODE (EPC): THE GLOBALIZATION OF ONE STANDARD AND THE CONSOLIDATION OF THAT CONTROL.

## BARCODES: HISTORICAL BACKGROUND

The marking of things began with the advent of barcodes. The Universal Product Code (UPC)[141] was the barcode symbology employed in the United States and Canada. The European Article Number (EAN) system[142] was the barcode symbology covering the rest of the world.

In 2004, the UCC and EAN International merged into a single global standards organization that covers 141 countries. The new organization is named GS1.[143] As of January 1, 2005,[144] all retail scanning systems around the world now accept the EAN-13 barcode symbology and GS1 controls the global standards.

GS1 has entered into a joint venture with GS1 US[145] to manage, expand, and standardize Electronic Product Code (EPC) technology. EPC is expected to replace the bar code as a means of marking objects. Unlike bar codes, EPC tags are capable of identifying each item manufactured, as opposed to just the manufacturer and class of products. Ultimately, EPCglobal is expected to create both a world-wide standard for RFID and the use of the Internet to share data via the EPCglobal Network.[146]

In summation, two significant events occurred during one twelve-month period from January 1, 2004 to January 1, 2005. First, the whole world switched over to a barcode structure that will allow the European barcodes to scan at point-of-sale in the rest of the world.[147] Secondly, the two entities that governed barcodes merged into one international organization called GS1. In short, one governing council (GS1) now controls the global standards for barcodes and the EPC. Finally, the United States Department of Homeland Security has proposed 2d barcodes [148] as the "common machine readable technology" for the United States' national identity card system.

# MEMO FROM THE DEVIL:
# PART 8—THE MARK OF THE BEAST

If you have ever wondered why the Most High referred to our next world leader as the Prince of the *Power of the Air* or why the rider of the white horse in the book of Revelation carries *a bow with no arrows*—he was alluding to our satellite-based network. Now that we are getting close you will realize why I have delegated assignments involving network responsibilities to various divisions with separate leaders. We had to keep these pieces separate before we put it all together or everyone would have understood what we were doing. We are about to begin the process of connecting each piece of the network. Each of these pieces all by themselves appears unrelated, mutually exclusive and relatively benign. However, once pieced together they will serve as the greatest system ever constructed.

Under current time constraints, I do not have time to go into extreme detail; however, here is a high-level summary. The network can be divided into several categories. First, the backbone of the network consists of the European Union's (EU) Galileo satellite system and the European Geostationary Navigation Overlay Service (EGNOS) ground system. Secondly, the fabric of the network consists of the Internet with its 13 root servers spread around the world. Thirdly, the appendages of the network are comprised of (a) toll booths which are equipped with Radio Frequency Identification (RFID) tag readers, (b) stationary RFID tag readers placed along highway infrastructure, (c) traffic light cameras, (d) retail loss prevention systems, and (e) point-of-sale (POS) devices. The glue that will hold all of these pieces together is the Electronic Product Code (EPC) utilizing wireless RFID technology.

For the mark of the beast we will utilize implantable RFID microchips. The protocols for pushing out the implantable microchips are finished and will be disseminated immediately after the rapture. I want the microchips inserted into the right hands of every human. Anyone missing a right hand or right arm (*i.e . . . amputees*) will receive the mark in their foreheads. The data demarcation between people who have a microchip in their hand versus those with microchips in their foreheads will be captured and coded differently within the system. We ran a barcode pilot project in the Dayton, Ohio area many years ago to iron out the wrinkles.

When this network is up and running you will be surprised at how seamless and ubiquitous it is. The key to this whole project is the EPC. Nobody seemed to notice the Sunrise Date on January 1, 2005. This was the date we set for all POS devices to accept the EAN-13 barcodes (*i.e . . . the EPC's predecessor*). In one day, we essentially switched the whole world over to an international commerce symbology system which accepts European barcodes, and it never popped up on anyone's radar. Amazing. A few months before that, we merged the UCC and EAN International into GS1. Again no one noticed. I was concerned that the timing proximity of the GS1 merger and the Sunrise Date would raise concerns with the Christ followers. They noticed nothing. This is proof positive that our apostasy efforts have yielded tremendous fruits. The EPC will act as the global standard for all commerce.

In case you have not connected the dots yet, once the network goes live and we have the implantable microchips in humans we will know everything. We will know the: who, what, when and where of every human activity and every item within commerce. Everything. We will know who buys what, where they purchased it and when. We will know where the product was manufactured, when it was shipped to a distribution facility and when it left for its retail destination. We will have a digital, real-time audit trail of every human's movements as well as their purchases. For example, we will be able to track (*in real time*) a single can of soda from the time it comes of the production line in Atlanta, Georgia to the time a consumer unloads their groceries in the driveway of their home in Memphis, Tennessee.

For years the manufacturers of POS hardware have installed RFID tag readers within their devices that consumers use to pay for items. (*i.e . . . the device at the check-out line that consumers swipe their credit cards on*). When a person approaches the check-out line at the grocery store they have no idea that the internal tag readers within the POS devices are activating the passive RFID tags on their person. This information is captured and logged for future use. In essence, the POS devices act as mini-toll booths that capture and store data on RFID tagged items. For years we have influenced retailers to ask for the zip codes of consumers at the POS. The true purpose of asking for zip codes is to add more geographic data to the system for future analysis and identification. Due to international database consolidation efforts we currently have *de facto* identifiers for the majority of the civilized world. Therefore, if you refuse to receive the mark of the beast we will still know where to find you. When the network comes on-line we will have absolute control of everything.

Finally, let me remind you of what is at risk. This high-stakes poker game we are about to play is one we cannot lose. We have pushed all our chips to the center of the table. I will not tolerate mistakes. You should execute your responsibilities with all due speed and be prepared for any *ad hoc* contingency plan instructions I issue, should they become necessary.

# CHAPTER TWELVE

# GLOBAL SATELLITE NAVIGATION

*". . . according to the prince of **the power of the air** . . ."Ephesians 2:2b NAS*

*"I looked, and behold, a white horse, and he who sat on it **had a bow** . . ." Revelation 6:2a NAS*

# Global Satellite Navigation (GNSS): Strategic Control Potential and the Privatization of that Control in the European Union's (EU's) Galileo Satellite System:

A satellite navigation system with global coverage is often referred to as a global navigation satellite system or GNSS. Currently, the European Union (EU) is developing a satellite system which they have named after Galileo.[149] The satellite system is a constellation of thirty (30) satellites and ground relay stations that has already cost the EU € 3.2 billion. EU member states have not contributed to the cost. Galileo was 100 percent funded through monies already appropriated in the EU's budget.

There are currently only two choices in the world for satellite navigational systems, the Global Positioning System (GPS)[150] owned by the United States and Global'naya Navigatsionnaya Sputnikovaya Sistema (GLONASS) the Global Navigation Satellite System [151] owned by Russia. Both systems are remnants of the cold war.

The problem with these two options (*from a consumer perspective*) is that service could be interrupted at any time. More specifically, when "civilian use" is at issue, access to the dominant system (GPS) could be severed by the U.S. Government. The EU is offering an alternative by offering unbroken service to civilian users and a roadmap to the future of satellite navigational systems. Some estimates of the economic and industrial development brought about by the Galileo system predict a 20 percent increase in the world satellite navigational market.[152]

In short, Galileo will have immediate applications in the transportation industry including road, rail and air freight management, air traffic control, and tracking cargo shipments. Aside from these more obvious applications, Galileo will have the capability of monitoring, reading, and interrogating RFID tags.

If Galileo did not exist, the widespread proliferation of RFID tags would still allow corporations to track anything consumers do. RFID "usefulness" is contingent upon it being "linked to a source of market or business intelligence such as inventory databases, demographic or psychographic markers. And the ability of RFID systems to enable the linking of product information with identity of a specific consumer is problematic without proper safeguards." [153]

The reality is that individual consumers are being linked to the products they buy via barcodes and RFID tags. At the checkout lines, consumers are frequently asked for their zip code, phone number, or other identifying information. Those links are captured in inventory databases, and demographic and psychographic markers. The individual databases and markers are being interlinked themselves through initiatives like TIA. Finally, the private sector in Europe will control Galileo. Very little attention has been given to the fact that this government-financed satellite system will be handed over to the private sector. The European private sector is guided by the motive for profit, as any other private sector entities. Galileo will monitor and track this consumer information.

# RFID AND TRANSPONDERS:

## *RFID SYSTEMS*

Radio-frequency identification or (RFID) systems may be roughly grouped into four categories: (1) electronic article surveillance (EAS) systems; (2) portable data capture systems; (3) networked systems; and (4) positioning systems.[154] EAS or Electronic Article Surveillance systems are usually used to sense the presence/absence of an item.[155] For example, most retail establishments have some form of RFID technology wherein a reader near the exit detects the presence of RFID tags on merchandise. Most people have witnessed another person leaving a store where the EAS alarm system beeps requiring the consumer to re-enter the store and open their shopping bag to prove they did not steal anything.

Portable data capture systems are handheld readers or portable data terminals that capture data, which is then transmitted directly to a host computer via a radio frequency link or held for delivery by line-linkage to the host.[156] Animal shelters use these hand-held readers to capture data in lost animals' microchips. Overnight mail delivery personnel scan packages as they are delivered so that the sender can track its progress online.

Networked systems applications are usually characterized by a fixed-position reader or readers,[157] which are connected directly to a networked information management system. Transponders are positioned on moving or movable items, or people, depending upon application. For example, a Walmart truck is filled with marked merchandise at the distribution center. As the truck passes by fixed-position readers on the highway, the computers in the Walmart headquarters know that the truck is on time, headed in the right direction, and carrying all of the merchandise.

Positioning systems, such as GPS devices, use transponders to facilitate automated location and navigation support for guided vehicles. Readers are positioned on the vehicles and linked to an onboard computer and radio frequency data communication (RFDC) link to the host information management system. Transponders that are programmed with identification and location information are embedded in the floor of the vehicle.[158]

## TRANSPONDERS

A transponder is a wireless communications control device that identifies and automatically responds to an incoming signal. (**Trans**mitter + Res**ponder** = **Transponder**). Generally, transponders may be either passive or active.

Transponders are considered passive if they do not contain their own power source. A passive transponder picks up power from, and must be used in conjunction with, an electric or magnetic field provided by a reader. Passive transponders are typically low cost, small, and seldom require battery changes. However, they have a relatively limited distance range.

Transponders are considered active if they contain their own power source. An active transponder will periodically transmit its identification and the reader will listen for any transponders in the nearby field. Active transponders have a relatively longer distance range than their passive counterparts. But they are larger, are more costly, and have a relatively short battery life. Active tags are good for asset and personnel tracking, as long as the cost can be justified. Currently, the cost generally ranges from $25 to $50.

## BIOMETRIC/HUMAN INTERFACE

Applied Digital Solutions, a Florida company, manufactures the VeriChip, a microchip designed to be implanted into humans. Applied Digital Solutions sought permission for the VeriChip from the Federal Communications Commission (FCC) because the chips use radio frequencies.[159]

Within four months of the request, the U.S. Food and Drug Administration (FDA) issued favorable guidance to Applied Digital Solutions,[160] ruling that it did not consider the device to be a "regulated medical device."[161] This ruling by the FDA cleared the way for the company to begin sales, marketing and distribution of VeriChip in the United States.[162]

Biometrics can be defined as *linking the distinguishing human anatomy to a single, confirmed biographical record*. The Greek word *bio* means *life* and *metric* means *measure*. Therefore, *biometric* means *life-measure*. For example, do the fingerprints (*distinguishing human anatomy*) of the person arrested match the name of the suspect John Q. Public who lives at 123 Main Street, Anytown USA (*single, confirmed biographical record*)?

*Distinguishing human anatomy* include (1) iris, (2) retinal, (3) face, (4) voice identification, (5) hand/finger geometry, and (6) fingerprints. A typical *single, confirmed biographical record* contains information including (1) name, (2) address, (3) date of birth, (4) social security number, (5) drivers' license number, (6) height, (7) eye color, (8) telephone number, (9) ethnicity, (10) sex, and (11) place of birth. Biometric systems are typically *pattern recognition systems* which are automated methods of determining the authenticity of a specific physiological or behavioral characteristic possessed by the subject to determine identity or verify identify.

Biometrics answers two critically important questions for millions of people on a daily basis: "Who is this person?"(*identification*) and "Is this person who they say they are?" (*verification*). Devices such as VeriChip allow distinguishing human anatomy to be *recorded* and *confirmed* for purposes of identification, and verification. Thus, implantable chips are poised to become the long-term solution for the biometric human interface issue.

## THE BIG 5 AND BRUSSELS, BELGIUM

The world is being changed by several institutions and the leaders of those entities. Five notable examples are (1) the country of Belgium, (2) the European Union's—Commission, (3) the European Union's—Council, (4) the European Union's—Parliament, and (5) GS1. I will refer to these as the "Big 5."

### *BELGIUM*

Belgium is widely regarded as the first country to embrace the concept of national identity cards, and is the world leader in the evolving technology. Other nations are looking to Belgium when they consider implementing this technological innovation. Belgium has implemented a national identity card system, and currently twenty of twenty-seven European Union nations have some form of a national identification card. Many EU countries sought advice from Belgium before implementing their own national identity card systems.

## THE EUROPEAN UNION (EU)

When the founding fathers of the EU signed the 1957 Treaty of Rome, they created a foundation (the European Economic Community or EEC) from which the current EU is built. The treaty created a common market and a European Parliament. The EEC also formed a European Commission that would formulate laws and regulations, harmonize tax codes, and reduce internal customs barriers.[163] When the Treaty of Rome was signed,[164] the Secretary General of the North Atlantic Treaty Organization (NATO) made an interesting statement. Paul-Henri Spaak stated, **"We felt like Romans on that day, we were conscientiously re-creating the Roman Empire once more."**[165] Not many people remember this statement. However, it is one piece of evidence that highlights the potential connection from the ancient prophecies of Daniel and the resurrection of the Roman Empire. Further, it signifies the relevance of Daniel's prophecy that the antichrist will come from the people who destroyed the temple (the Romans).[166]

The EU is comprised of three primary bodies, the (1) Council,[167] (2) Parliament,[168] and the (3) Commission.[169] The foundation of the European Union lies within its foundational treaties, accession treaties, and its amending treaties. The EU is comprised of approximately 494 million citizens.[170] The European Union currently possesses one of the world's largest growing economies with an estimated gross domestic product (GDP) of 15.2 trillion USD.[171]

The EU now has a constitution unifying the EU member states (*or the revived Roman Empire*). The Treaty of Lisbon was signed on December 13, 2007, and it entered into force on December 1, 2009.

GS1 is now the single governing council of global standards for the barcode industry in 141 countries. Brussels, Belgium is the geographical center of activity for many of the participating institutions. The GS1 Global Headquarters,[172] the Council for the European Union,[173] and the Parliament for the EU,[174] are located in Brussels, and are within close proximity. The European Commission also has its headquarters and at least fifty-one (51) other locations in Brussels, Belgium.[175]

These five entities (Country of Belgium, EU Council, EU Parliament, EU Commission, and the GS1) are poised to change the world significantly. They possess one of the world's largest economies, and their headquarters are geographically situated within the same city. Commercial revenues from satellite navigation are increasing at twenty percent (20 percent) per year.[176] The revenues from the satellite navigation industry went from very small in 2001 to $12 billion in 2002 and $24.9 billion in 2006.[177] According to EU estimates annual gross revenues for satellite navigation products are estimated to be over $300 billion dollars by the year 2020.[178] The EU is in position to control much of the future global satellite navigation industry. The EU has the infrastructure to affect *de facto* control, centralized in one city, over the future of global commerce.

## THE HUMAN MOTIVE: MONEY

Pascal Campagne, CEO of France Développement Conseil (FDC) "is in charge of satellite navigation activities, including coordinating studies and development and consultancy projects for the European Commission, European Space Agency, and the French Ministries of Transport, Defence, and Space."[179] He stated that *"the EU's development of the infrastructure and specifications of Galileo will clearly give them the upper hand in steering the choice of products and services they are intending to develop."*[180]

Laurent Gauthier, EGNOS Project Manager for the European Space Agency (ESA) stated, *"EGNOS improves the precision and availability of the information and is a precursor to Galileo. It allows a wide range of applications to benefit from this precision and allows industry to obtain a foothold in this booming market."*[181] For anyone paying attention it appears that these five entities are on the verge of monopolizing an entire industry (global commerce) that will extend into every area of human life.

When the world is ready to move from barcodes to the EPC, the EU will be in position to further its vision of the Internet. Most people have not asked the question about motive. For those who have—the purely human motivation pertaining to the development of Galileo and EGNOS is pecuniary. Clearly, there is a financial benefit to owning a satellite system and accompanying ground system that can detect, identify, and globally monitor EPC tags in real time. The furthering of this vision will provide financial benefits to the EU and its private sector by knowing the *what, where,* and *when* of everything marked with an EPC tag. The true purpose of this infrastructure is absolute control not mere financial gain.

## EUROPEAN CORPORATIONS IN THE USA

In 2005, the Texas Transportation Commission selected a Spanish firm, Madrid-based Cintra, Concesiones de Infraestructuras de Transporte, S.A., (Cintra) to build and operate a 316-mile leg of the Trans-Texas Corridor that would bypass Interstate 35 from San Antonio to north of Dallas-Fort Worth.[182] Cintra proposed to build this highway within five years at no cost to the state.[183] Cintra offered to contribute over $7 billion in tollway infrastructure in exchange for the right to collect tolls for fifty years.[184] Cintra is already reading the toll tags on Tollway 130 in Central Texas. This toll road is currently the only private-public roadway project in progress in Central Texas.[185] The Trans-Texas Corridor project never got approved.

The media and the politicians erroneously formulated the issues. Ultimately, the deal never got done. The issue was framed as one of *whether we should allow a foreign corporation to operate an American toll way.* Stakeholders, politicians, and the public actually believed Cintra was willing to pay for $7 billion worth of highway infrastructure so they could recapture their investment one quarter at a time. Nobody who offers that kind of value does so solely with the intent of collecting it in change hoping they will recoup their investment over 20 years or more. What Cintra was really after was the information. In short, due to the advent of RFID tags on products in the supply chain, and since Cintra would be operating the toll tag readers, they could also read RFID tags on any vehicles—they would possess all information of anything moving along the toll ways (i.e. what is inside each 18-wheeler truck, how many cartons of X, when it entered the country, where it was going, what time it left point X, etc.). This is a strategic model employed by the EU for control purposes. If the EU private sector can get a foothold in controlling American commerce; they will be one step closer to where they are headed with controlling global commerce and ultimately the mark of the beast.

Existing toll roads use RFID technology at the toll booths. Cintra is headquartered in Madrid, Spain.[186] Cintra's offices are located less than twelve miles from the Madrid suburb of Torrejon, which is home to one of the EGNOS/Galileo Satellite master control facilities.[187] This is yet another geographic anomaly that has gone unnoticed by most.

# CHAPTER THIRTEEN

# CLOUD COMPUTING

*It also forced all people, great and small, rich and poor, free and slave, to receive a mark on their right hands or on their foreheads, so that they could not buy or sell unless they had the mark, which is the name of the beast or the number of its name. Revelation 13:16-17*

# CLOUD COMPUTING: THE EUROPEAN UNION'S PLAN "B" TO OBTAIN CONTROL OF THE INTERNET

Cloud computing is a new delivery and consumption model for information technology (IT) services based on the Internet. It could also be defined as the use of Internet-based services to support a business process. Oftentimes it involves the provision of dynamically scalable and virtualized resources.

Currently there are three different forms of cloud computing. First, there is a "Public Cloud," where services are sold to anyone on the Internet. Second, there is a "Private Cloud," which is a proprietary network or data center supplying hosted services to a limited number of people. Third, there is a "Virtual Private Cloud" where public cloud services are used to create a private cloud.

The distinctiveness of cloud computing or its characteristics that make it distinguishable from typical hosted services, are threefold. These characteristics are it is:

1. <u>Sold on Demand</u>: i.e. by the minute or by the hour
2. <u>Elastic</u>: the user can have as much or as little as it desires
3. <u>Fully Managed by the Provider</u>: the user merely needs a PC and Internet access

Currently there are three basic services that cloud computing providers offer:

1. <u>Infrastructure as a Service</u>: (aka "utility computing") *"pay for what you use"* model, similar to electricity or water and sewage.
2. <u>Platform as a Service</u>: software and product development tools are hosted on provider's infrastructure (* no standards)

3. <u>Software as a Service</u>: provider hosts the application and the data; provider provides hardware infrastructure and software.

# TANGIBLE BENEFITS OF **RFID** TECHNOLOGIES

-Access Control

-Asset Management

-Asset Tracking

-Automobile Tracking: in auto rental industry

-Blood Analysis Identification

-Car Body Production

-Container/Pallet Tracking

-Duty Evasion

-Fleet Maintenance: and tire tracking

-Food Production Control

-Gas Bottle Inventory Control

-Grocery store checkout

-Healthcare

-ID Badges and Access Control

-Inventory Control

-Library

-Livestock: tracking and linking the animal to food, location

-Machine Tool Management

-Manufacturing: tracking of parts during manufacture, tracking of assembled items

-Medical Applications: linking a patient with key drugs, personnel giving the drugs, biometric measurements

-Medical Equipment Personnel Tracking

-Military

-Military Logistics

-Oil Pipe Identification

-Parking Lot Access and control

-Parts Identification

-People Tracking: security tracking for entrance management or security, contact management at events, baby tags in hospitals to manage access to postnatal wards

-Person Identification

-Pharmacy

-Product Tracking: from manufacture through assembly

-Production Line Monitoring

-Refuse Collection Identification

-Retail: tracking shopping carts in supermarkets, active shelves

-Retail Security

-Road Construction Material Identification

-Security: Attorney General's Office in Mexico

-Security Guard Monitoring

-Stolen Vehicle Identification

-Supply Chain Automation: the key early driver for developments and implementation of the technology

-Timber Grade Monitoring

-Timing: in sports events

-Toll Tags

-Tracking Currency

-Toxic Waste Monitoring

-Valuable Objects Insurance Identification

-Vehicle Parking Monitoring

-Warehouses: real-time inventory

-Water Analysis

-Wireless Payment[188]

# MEMO FROM THE DEVIL: PART 9 — GNSS AND CLOUD COMPUTING

As we have previously discussed during principality and power meetings—"control of the Internet" is of paramount importance to fulfilling our mission and seeing our vision into reality. As a point of re-emphasis, "control of the Internet" can be summarized in five key areas: (1) who operates the database of generic names, (2) who appoints the operators for two-letter country code suffixes, (3) who decides Internet Protocol number allocation, (4) who controls the root servers, and (5) who establishes the technical standards.[189] As I was strategizing a few years ago I asked myself the following question, *"Is our goal to get the United States to relinquish control of the Internet to Europe so we can obtain the information we need? Or is our true goal to merely obtain the information we need?"* That is when I came up with the idea of cloud computing. SEE TABLE—*USA* AND *EU* SECTORS

|  | United States of America (USA) | European Union (EU) |
|---|---|---|
| **Private Sector** | **Sector 1:**<br><br>-Not even at the table when control of the Internet is discussed | **Sector 2:** in the future will control<br><br>-Galileo Satellite System<br><br>-EGNOS Ground System |
| **Public Sector (Governmental)** | **Sector 3:**<br><br>-Controls GPS<br><br>-Controls the Internet | **Sector 4:**<br><br>-Currently building Galileo & EGNOS |

**Chart 7: Cloud Computing—USA and EU Sectors**

If we cannot get control of the Internet from Sector 3 into Sector 2 where we need it, why don't we just wrest control of the information itself vis-à-vis cloud computing. Sector 1 will support it because it will financially benefit them through (1) cost savings as well as (2) increased revenues. Once they have access to the information, they can use it for research and development and marketing. Not to mention that Sector 1 did not even have a voice on the issue in years past. Sector 2 will like it because it will give them the upper hand in developing products that it intends to manufacture. In a nutshell, "market share" = more money. Sectors 1 and 2 are probably both smart enough to recognize that in the foreseeable future Sector 2 will eventually monopolize all the information anyway by virtue of Galileo & EGNOS. Sector 4 does not have anything to lose (*or so they think until we are through using them to create a New World Order*). Sector 3 can't stop us because it's Sectors 1 and 2 that are selling cloud computing services. Let's keep this movement going and **DO NOT** allow influential entities to entertain the following questions:

-*Why should we just give up our Information Technology (IT) infrastructure?*
-*What assurances are there to ensure that the people who control this information are in fact trustworthy?*

In summary, we could not get the US to relinquish control of the Internet and to share that control voluntarily. However, we will accomplish that goal through Plan "B"—cloud computing. I get what I want to fulfill my vision and mission. I just had to resort to Plan "B" to accomplish it. Either way I win.

# CHAPTER FOURTEEN

## CONCLUSIONS

*For God did not appoint us to suffer wrath but to receive salvation through our Lord Jesus Christ. 1 Thessalonians 5:9*

# WHERE THE WORLD IS HEADED WITH RFID AND EPC

We can expect an interconnected digital world where anonymity will soon become a relic of the past. The days of people not knowing *who* you are, *where* you are and *when* you were there . . . are over. The implementation of marking and tracking technologies has a price tag, and anonymity is part of the cost.

Biometrics is a *task* and RFID is a *technology*. The location where these two overlap is a clear picture of the New World Order and your future should you choose to reject Jesus Christ. The future of biometrics (*linking the distinguishing human anatomy to a single, confirmed biographical record*) will have multifaceted benefits. However, be cautious of merely focusing upon the tangible, socially acceptable benefits which include fighting terrorism, crime, and addressing illegal immigration. From a forensic perspective these movements will provide key evidence in most criminal investigations. More specifically, the first three elements of every crime—(1) the identity of the defendant, (2) the date the crime occurred, and (3) jurisdiction (*i.e. where the crime occurred—county and state*)—can be proved up with this new evidence when it is available.

Notwithstanding the aforementioned pragmatic benefits, our society needs to keep their eye on the bigger picture. The legal world and homeland security will need to understand where these movements intersect with their responsibilities. For example, prosecutors and criminal investigators will have to become familiar with this evidence, so they will know where to send the subpoenas to obtain the evidence. This will require law enforcement agencies to systematically categorize (1) the entity (or entities) that possess the evidence, (2) the type of evidence/records, (3) the systems that contain this evidence, (4) who the custodians of records are, and (5) to whom the subpoenas are to be sent. This will be required for law enforcement agencies to obtain the pertinent evidence. Aside from these relatively narrow societal benefits, never forget *what* is occurring and more importantly *why*.

The erosion of national sovereignty does not always occur in the spotlight. Sometimes the most dangerous developments occur slowly and quietly. Erosion is a subtle, vicious enemy. It would be wise to be wary of formulating the issues in relatively narrow beneficial terms. We do need to recognize that there are three problems that are not going away: (1) crime (*tyranny from within*), (2) terrorism (*tyranny from the outside*), and (3) illegal immigration. However, globalization is changing the dynamics of many things in our world. The salient issues at hand are not what merely benefit us as a society. These changes must be understood through the paradigm of a triangle of multiple movements that are (1) marking people, (2) marking things, and (3) establishing the monitoring capabilities of those marks. The triangle of these movements poses itself as a partial solution to the problems of crime, terrorism, and illegal immigration. The fuel propelling these movements is two divergent visions of what the Internet will become. The internet will one day become a world wide web of all things because the real end game is the control of global commerce vis-à-vis the mark of the beast.

Finally, you can expect an interconnected digital world where (1) people are marked by the proliferation of EPC-marked implantable microchips utilizing RFID technology, (2) everything else in the world will be marked with an EPC RFID tag, and (3) those EPC code structures will be monitored by Galileo and its ground system EGNOS. The Big 5's physical presence in the same town (*Brussels, Belgium*) is not a geographic coincidence. It is part of a larger plan to obtain control of global commerce. One of the last impediments between the Big 5 and its vision of a uniform, digitally interconnected world of all things is the control of the Internet. The EU was unsuccessful in their attempts to have the United States voluntarily relinquish control of the Internet so the EU could obtain the information they desired. *Cloud computing* appears to be the EU's newest strategy to obtain control of the information, notwithstanding the United States' refusal to cooperate.

## CLOSING THOUGHTS

Satan is a deadly adversary. He will *eat your sack lunch* and then pop the bag. However, he is not your only enemy. Our fleshly desires (*human depravity*) and Satan's world system (*the cosmos*) form the other two edges of this dangerous trio. Today we live in a *world of gray*, where situational ethics and no absolutes are the menu favorites. People today do not want to hear anything about judgment or consequences for their actions. Jesus apparently thought differently. In Luke 11:23 and Matthew 12:30 Jesus stated, *"Whoever is not with me is against me, and whoever does not gather with me scatters."* According to Jesus we are either with him or against him. We are either helping him or opposing him. If you sincerely disagree with Jesus, you are sincerely wrong.

I laugh to myself in the courthouses I walk through when I hear people talking about what they will do when they get their *day in court*. They have no idea, ostensibly from watching too much television. The real courtroom is a rude slap in the face for many. People quickly realize they are not in charge, the judge is. They realize they cannot even speak out loud until procedure allows it. Their attorney-advocate speaks for them. Oftentimes, it is not a pretty picture. The harsh reality is you fall into one of two groups. Either you (1) have accepted Jesus Christ as your Savior by confessing with your mouth and believing in your heart that Jesus in Lord and God raised him from the dead, or (2) you have not. If you are in the second group, you have a choice to make. Do you want to stand before God in judgment at the formal sentencing of the Great White Throne judgment? Or do you want Jesus as your advocate with the Father? The conscious choice you make about Jesus will determine whether you become a child of God, or whether you stand before him in his capacity as a judge.

I created a website (www.give-an-answer.com) that should answer some of your basic questions regarding salvation. As an attorney, I just want you to make an informed decision. It frustrates me when people accuse me of *wanting everyone to think like me*. I really don't. The world would be very boring if everyone was like me—just ask my friends. I truly value differences. My goal is to share the gospel so whatever decision people make, is an informed decision. It is the Holy Spirit's job to convict the world of sin, righteous and judgment according to John 16:8-11. As another sinner saved by grace, I'm not qualified to convict people of sin, righteous and judgment. Since God put those responsibilities in his job description, I do not venture there.

God loves you and has a plan for your life. That plan can only be received at the foot of the cross. Jesus's gracious offer of salvation is free. It costs absolutely nothing because Jesus already paid for it. It is free. No charge. Once you become a believer you will need to (1) *fear God*, which means to take him seriously, and (2) *obey God*, which means to do what he says. Once you become a believer the Holy Spirit will endow you with a spiritual gift or a series of spiritual gifts. Then he will call you to do something for him. That is when you need to put your seatbelt on. It is a shock to move from the spectator stands onto the playing field, but that is where the action is. That is also where you will find our Lord. I bear the scars of someone who has seen some playing time, but I would not trade those cuts and bruises for anything.

I enjoy people because they are so interesting. Honestly, I do not believe I love most people enough to die for them. Facing death will reveal your true character. One month after I graduated from high school I was shot at by some bank robbers fleeing the scene of a robbery that I had witnessed. I bravely jumped underneath a car trying to save my own skin. That makes me a coward, not a savior. Further, I would never allow my 12-year old son to be slaughtered and ridiculed in order to have a relationship with people. Especially since I know going in, many of those would not want to have a relationship with me. However, there is a God that loves you that much. He shed his own blood at a public execution where he was ridiculed and beaten for the sins we now choose to commit.

**To receive that free offer from God merely requires that you confess with your mouth and believe in your heart—that Jesus is who he claimed to be**. If confessional, repentant words like these have never emanated from your heart and through your lips, you had better take a long look in the mirror. In a world that does not offer free lunches, it is the only offer I've ever seen that really is free. It is free. On the house. No cost. Free of charge. Gratis. Ironically, that **free gift** is the only thing that will **set you free** to become the person God intended you to be.

# MEMO FROM THE DEVIL: PART 10 — GOING FORWARD

Our work plan going forward continues to require your unified and synergistic efforts that leverage all three enemies, executing our three primary strategies, to produce four behaviors, resulting from four primary desires emanating from the four component parts of the human heart, the center of which is the human mind. This is why we target the human mind.

For review humans have three enemies (1) me, (2) the world, and (3) the flesh or human depravity. We leverage these enemies with three primary strategies: (1) lust of the flesh, (2) lust of the eyes, and the (3) boastful pride of life. I used all three of these strategies on Eve in the Garden of Eden and on Jesus in the wilderness. These strategies have proven to be extremely effective in producing a progressive linear behavioral cycle of (1) depravity ⇨ (2) permissiveness, ⇨ (3) rationalization, and ⇨ (4) sin.[190] This sequential behavioral cycle emanates from at least one of four human desires (1) fame, (2) fortune, (3) power, and/or (4) pleasure.[191] These desires (*and everything else a human does*) flow from the human heart. The human heart has four component parts: (1) the conscience, (2) emotions, (3) the will, and (4) the mind at the center. See the chart I have created for your review.

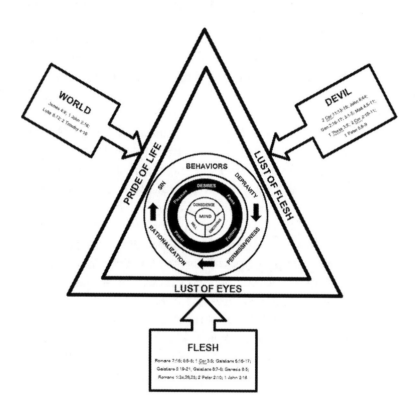

**Chart 8: Summary of Enemies, Strategies, Behaviors, Desires and Human Heart**

This work plan continues to be effective for many reasons, not the least of which is their ignorance of some basic understandings. First, humans do not know what their "heart" is. Therefore they cannot follow the greatest commandment to *"Love the Lord your God with all your heart . . . and with all your strength.* Secondly, this ignorance inhibits their ability to follow an equally important and material commandment to *"Above all else, guard your heart."* Thirdly, they are ignorant to the fact that their own hearts are the most deceitful part of themselves. As the bad book says, *"The 'heart' is deceitful above all things and beyond cure."* The humans' blindness to these three truths will thankfully prevent them from being set free. I love it when I hear them misquote the Bible by saying *"the truth will set you free."* Humans are blind to the fact that Jesus said, *"If you hold to my teaching . . . then you will know the truth, and the truth will set you free."* They simply do not know that **obedience** produces **knowledge of the truth** and that knowledge has the ability to **set them free.**

Stay focused on our vision and mission. We must work together to accomplish our goals. The synergistic impact of our collective focus is the only hope we have to escape the lake of fire. God asks his sheep to forgive others. In fact he demands it. However, he will not forgive us. I told him once that was hypocritical, when I was accusing Christ followers in his presence. His response had something to do with *our character* being permanently altered. Whatever! I tell you that to dissuade you from any expectations of sympathy or mercy. Neither will be forthcoming.

Our Vision Statement reads, *"We must exterminate the Jewish race of humans, thereby, making it impossible for God to fulfill his stated promises to the Jews. Once they are eradicated, he will be a proven liar and one of two things will occur. Either:*

*(1) He will suspend His sentence upon us to spend eternity in the lake of fire, or*

*(2) He will experience another rebellion in heaven as the remaining angels in heaven who witness his failed promises firsthand, rise up against him like we did not so long ago."*

As we move forward to realize this vision we will continue to employ our primary strategy of defrauding humanity. Our Mission Statement reads,

> *Utilizing our primary tool of 'fraud' (intentional deception or intentional misrepresentation), **target the minds of unbelievers and Christ followers**. Lead them astray from the purity and simplicity of devotion to Jesus Christ. Minimize, mitigate, and neutralize the straightforwardness of the gospel message through every available means. Ensure that our counterfeit explanations are appealing, attractive, encouraging, caring, intelligent and plausible.*

Stay focused on our priorities. It is all about body count. There is nothing quite like the look on a human's face when they arrive in Hell and realize two things (1) they are there because they rejected Christ, and (2) they are never leaving. It is truly priceless to witness their unmitigated horror. Remember what you are here for. Now more than ever you must stay focused on the task at hand and work together.

I am especially pleased with your efforts in regards to the unbelievers *who think* they are Christ followers. Most of these church-going, good people have been deceived with intellectual assent. They intellectually state their belief in God; however, they have never believed in their hearts. The biggest tool we have in our arsenal is the human heart. I'm not referring to the muscle that beats in the chests of humans. I'm referring to the *heart (the center and seat of their lives)*. It is there that you will find their minds, wills, emotions, and consciences.

<u>Continue blinding them to the following truths</u>:

1.  The human heart is deceitful above all things, even me.
2.  To become a true Christ follower they must believe in their hearts. Repentance (*or a changing of the mind*) is an integral and necessary part of believing.[192] This keeps people from becoming Christ followers.

The rapture of Christ followers is imminently approaching. Gear up and let's bring the heat!

# ABOUT THE AUTHOR

Bart Bevers is a lawyer in Texas. Mr. Bevers is the former Inspector General at the Office of Inspector General (OIG) in Texas, where he ran the largest state OIG in the nation. He served seven years at the OIG and nine years as an Assistant District Attorney. He has specialized in fraud and white-collar crime. As the chief prosecutor in five different courts and a civil litigator, Mr. Bevers has personally tried over 450 contested trials in criminal and civil courts.

Mr. Bevers currently serves on the Board of Regents for the Association of Certified Fraud Specialists (ACFS), the Board of Directors for the Association of Inspectors General (AIG), and is an instructor for the National White Collar Crime Center (NW3C). He is certified as a Certified Fraud Examiner (C.F.E.), Certified Fraud Specialist (C.F.S.), Certified Homeland Security, Level III (C.H.S-III), Certified Inspector General (C.I.G.) and Certified Public Manager (CPM). Mr. Bevers is also licensed to practice law in Texas.

Mr. Bevers was the recipient of the 2009 Public Administrator of the Year in Texas by the American Society for Public Administration (ASPA), and nationally recognized with the 2008 Sentinel Award by the Association of Certified Fraud Specialists in San Francisco, California.

Mr. Bevers became a Christ follower over thirty-eight years ago at age nine. He has been married to his best friend for sixteen years and has two children, a son and a daughter. He is an avid golfer, and enjoys running—even in the Texas heat.

# CHAPTER ONE:

1.     Ezekiel Chapter 28:11-19

2.     Ezekiel 28:13

3.     Ezekiel 28:14

4.     Ezekiel 28:14

5.     Ezekiel 28:15

6.     Genesis 3:1-7

7.     1 Timothy 3:6

8.     Job 1:6-12

9.     Ezekiel 28:12

10.     Ezekiel 28:14

11.     Ezekiel 28:16

12.     *Hebrew and Chaldee Dictionary, The Hebrew-Greek Key Study Bible* (AMG Publishers, 1990). James Strong, S.T.D., L.L.D. [*rakal* (raw-kal'); a prim. root; to travel for trading:—(spice) merchant].

13.     Job 1:7

14.     1 Peter 5:8

15.     Ezekiel 28:12

16.     Isaiah 14:13-14

[17]    Revelation 12:4 (He swept 1/3 of stars from sky with his tail)

[18]    Genesis 3:1

[19]    *Hebrew and Chaldee Dictionary, The Hebrew-Greek Key Study Bible* (AMG Publishers, 1990). James Strong, S.T.D., L.L.D. [*rakal* (raw-kal'); a prim. root; to travel for trading:—(spice) merchant].

[20]    Id.

[21]    The Rolling Stones, "Sympathy for the Devil" (1968).


## CHAPTER TWO:

[22]    Romans 10:9

[23]    *The Millennium,* by Lorraine Boettner [Nutley, N.J.: Presbyterian and Reformed, 1957], p. 14.

[24]    *Basic Theology,* by Charles Ryrie p. 445 [6th edition 1988].

[25]    Id. at 450

[26]    1,000 years as mentioned in Revelation 20

[27]    1 Thess. 4:16—5:2

[28]    2 Peter 3:10

[29]    1 Corinthians 4:1-2,5

[30]    James 1:27; James 4:4; 1 John 2:16-17; Luke 8:12; 2 Timothy 4:10; 1 John 5:19

[31]    Matthew 7:15-20; Matthew 12:33

# CHAPTER FOUR:

[32]  Matthew 24:8; Mark 13:8;

[33]  Matthew 24:36, 25:13; Mark 13:32

[34]  Revelation 16:17-21(KJV): Verse 21 states, "*From the sky huge hailstones, each weighing about a talent, fell on people. And they cursed God on account of the plague of hail, because the plague was so terrible.*" The stones will weigh between 57 and 130 pounds each. (*depending on what God meant when he used the word "talent"*).

Talent Weight Measurement:
Greek Talent = 26 kilograms (57 lb)
Roman Talent = 32.3 kilograms (71 lb)
Egyptian Talent = 27 kilograms (60 lb)
Babylonian Talent = 30.3 kilograms (67 lb)
Heavy Common Talent = 58.9 kilograms (130 lb) [*probably used in Palestine during New Testament times*]

[35]  http://earthquake.usgs.gov/earthquakes/eqinthenews.

[36]  2 Thessalonians 2:10b-11 NIV: "*They perish because they refused to love the truth and so be saved. For this reason **God sends them a powerful delusion** so that they will believe the lie [12] and so that all will be condemned who have not believed the truth but have delighted in wickedness.*"

[37]  Luke 21:24b NIV: "*Jerusalem will be trampled underfoot by the Gentiles until the times of the Gentiles be fulfilled.*"

[38]  Matthew 24:14 NIV: "*And this gospel of the kingdom will be preached in the whole world as a testimony to all nations, and then the end will come.*"39     Proverbs 6:6 NIV: "*Go to the ant, you sluggard; consider its ways and be wise!*"

## CHAPTER EIGHT:

[40]  The American Heritage Dictionary (2nd College Edition) p. 115 [ME *Antecrist*<OFr. < Med. Lat. *Antichristus*<Llat. < Gk. *Antikristos:anti-*, opposed to + *khristos*, anointed.—see Christ.] Houghton Mifflin Company, 1982.

[41]  Revelation 13:2

[42]  Ezekiel 28:16


## CHAPTER NINE:

[43]  Matthew 6:33 KJV: *"Seek ye first the kingdom of God and his righteousness, and all these things shall be added unto you."*

[44]  Daniel 7:8, 11, 19-21

[45]  Daniel 8:9-14

[46]  Daniel 8:23-25; 11:36

[47]  Daniel 9:26-27

[48]  Daniel 9:27

[49]  Matthew 24:15; Mark 13:14

[50]  John 5:43

[51]  2 Thessalonians 2:3

[52]  1 John 2:18; 4:3

[53]  2 John 7

54    Revelation 6:2

55    Revelation 13:2; 14:9; 16:13; 17:10-13; 19:19-20; 20:10

56    2 Thessalonians 2:3

57    Matthew 11:27; 28:18

58    John 5:43

59    John 5:19-23

60    Matthew 6:9

61    1 John 2:1

62    John 14:16 (He will give you another helper)

63    Revelation 16:13

64    Genesis 3:1,4-5

65    Matthew 4:1-11; Luke 4:1-13

66    Revelation 13:11-12

67    Revelation 13:13

68    Acts 2:3

69    Revelation 13:16

70    Ephesians 1:13-14; 4:30; Revelation 9:4

71    Revelation 13:4

72    Psalms 66:4

73    Ephesians 4:6

74    John 8:44

75    Psalms 11:4

76    Isaiah 14:13-14

77    2 Thessalonians 2:9

78    2 Thessalonians 2:4

79    Revelation 13:3,12

80    Revelation 13:14

81    John 19:34

82    Revelation 17:8

## CHAPTER TEN:

83    1 John 4:3

84    1 John 4:2

85    2 Thessalonians 2:2

86    2 Thessalonians 2:3

87    "Third Millennium Teens, Research on the Minds, Hearts and Souls of America's Teenagers", page 44, Barna Research Group, Ltd. 1999

88    Id.

89    2 Thessalonians 2:3

90    John F. Walvoord and Roy B. Zuck, *The Bible Knowledge Commentary* (Colorado Springs, CO, Cook Communications Ministries 2000), 718.

91    2 Thessalonians 2:5-7

92    1 John 2:18

93    Daniel 2:36-38

94    Daniel 2:40-43

95    Daniel 7:23

96    Daniel 7:5

97    Daniel 7:17

98    Daniel 7:23

99    Daniel 2:40-43

100    Daniel 2:40-41

101    Daniel 9:26

102    Matthew 24:1-2

# CHAPTER ELEVEN:

[103]   Philip Willan, The Guardian, "Silvio Berlusconi's report card," May 15, 2002 http://www.guardian.co.uk/elsewhere/journalist/story/0,7792,715851,00.html.

[104]   www.governo.it (The Prime Minister's Agenda and International Engagements).

[105]   James Fox, The Guardian, "First Among Billionaires," September 28, 2002, http://www.guardian.co.uk/italy/story/0,12576,824146,00.html.

[106]   "Silvio Berlusconi, self-styled man of the people," by Francesca Caferri, CNN Italy, 2001 http://www.cnn.com/SPECIALS/2001/italy/stories/berlusconi/.

[107]   James Fox, The Guardian, September 28, 2002, http://www.guardian.co.uk/italy/story/0,12576,824146,00.html.

[108]   BBC World News, November 15, 2000, "Mirth and anger at Berlusconi 'miracle'" by David Willey in Rome, http://news.bbc.co.uk/1/hi/world/europe/1025545.stm.

[109]   Bloomberg News, October 9, 2002.

[110]   Gail Edmondson, BusinessWeek, October 22, 2001, "Commentary: Berlusconi's Accidental Gift to Bin Laden,"http://ad.doubleclick.net/adi/N3166.BusinessWeek/B1102547;sz=1x1;ord=5460486.616505466%3f.

[111]   www.wikipedia.org.

[112]   Id.

[113] World Socialist We Site, "Italy's Berlusconi and his 'House of Freedoms'—a new dimension in the development of the right wing in Europe," by Peter Schwarz, May 7, 2001. http://www.wsws.org/articles/2001/may2001/ital-m07.shtml.

[114] James Fox, The Guardian, "First Among Billionaires," September 28, 2002, http://www.guardian.co.uk/italy/story/0,12576,824146,00.html.

[115] Askmen.com, "Silvio Berlusconi," March 9, 2003, http://www.askmen.com/men/business_politics/47c_silvio_berlusconi.html.

[116] Askmen.com, "Silvio Berlusconi," March 9, 2003, http://www.askmen.com/men/business_politics/47c_silvio_berlusconi.html.

[117] The Los Angeles Times, "Berlusconi New Italian Premier Indictments, Fickle Allies Are Potential Pitfalls for New PM", by Richard Boudreaux May 15, 2001. (Volume 121, Number 26) http://the-tech.mit.edu/V121/N26/italy.26w.html.

[118] Rory Carroll, The Guardian International, "Italy's Houdini poised to pull off his greatest trick," Saturday December 16, 2000, http://www.guardian.co.uk/Netgravity/popup5/0,,00.html?IFRHEIGHT="200"?IFRWIDTH="200"?IFRAMEB GCOL="000000"?SPACEDESC=popupbig1.

[119] Askmen.com, "Silvio Berlusconi," March 9, 2003, http://www.askmen.com/men/business_politics/47c_silvio_berlusconi.html.

[120] Askmen.com, "Silvio Berlusconi," March 9, 2003, http://www.askmen.com/men/business_politics/47c_silvio_berlusconi.html.

[121]   James Fox, The Guardian, "First Among Billionaires," September 28, 2002, http://www.guardian.co.uk/italy/story/0,12576,824146,00.html.

[122]   CNN, 2001, by Francesca Caferri, "Silvio Berlusconi, self-styled man of the people," http://www.cnn.com/SPECIALS/2001/italy/stories/berlusconi/.

[123]   Philip Willan, The Guardian, "Fans of Berlusconi Reveal Nobel intent," September 4, 2002, http://www.guardian.co.uk/international/story/0,3604,785592,00.html.

[124]   BBC News, David Willey, "Italian boycott over euro price hikes," July 5, 2002, http://news.bbc.co.uk/1/hi/world/europe/2100991.stm.

[125]   The Palestine Chronicle, March 17, 2002.

[126]   Rory Carroll, The Guardian International, "Italy's Houdini poised to pull off his greatest trick," Saturday December 16, 2000, http://www.guardian.co.uk/Netgravity/popup5/0,,,00.html?IFRHEIGHT="200"?IFRWIDTH="200"?IFRAMEB GCOL= "000000"?SPACEDESC=popupbig1.

[127]   Rory Carroll, The Guardian International, "Italy's Houdini poised to pull off his greatest trick," Saturday December 16, 2000, http://www.guardian.co.uk/Netgravity/popup5/0,,,00.html?IFRHEIGHT="200"?IFRWIDTH="200"?IFRAMEB GCOL= "000000"?SPACEDESC=popupbig1.

[128]   BBC World News, November 15, 2000, "Mirth and anger at Berlusconi 'miracle,'" by David Willey in Rome, http://news.bbc.co.uk/1/hi/world/europe/1025545.stm.

[129]   Philip Willan, The Guardian, "Fans of Berlusconi Reveal Nobel intent," September 4, 2002, http://www.guardian.co.uk/international/story/0,3604,785592,00.html.

## CHAPTER THIRTEEN:

[130]   Matthew 12:34

[131]   Revelation 13:8, 12, 16-18; Matthew 24:15; 2 Thessalonians 2:3-8

[132]   "Biometrics" for the purposes of this communication is defined as "linking the distinguishing human anatomy of a person to a single, confirmed biographical record."

[133]   *"Who Will Control the Internet?" by Kenneth Neil Cukier, Foreign Affairs, published by the Council on Foreign Affairs November/ December 2005, Vol 84, Number 6.*

[134]   Id. <u>DEPARTMENT OF COMMERCE</u>: National Telecommunications and Information Administration, June 30, 2005.

*Domain Names: U.S. Principles on the Internet's Domain Name and Addressing System*
The United States Government intends to preserve the security and stability of the Internet's Domain Name and Addressing System (DNS). Given the Internet's importance to the world's economy, it is essential that the underlying DNS of the Internet remain stable and secure. As such, the United States is committed to taking no action that would have the potential to adversely impact the effective and efficient operation of the DNS and will therefore maintain its historic role in authorizing changes or modifications to the authoritative root zone file.

Governments have legitimate interest in the management of their country code top level domains (ccTLD). The United States recognizes that governments have legitimate public policy and sovereignty concerns with respect to the management of their ccTLD. As such, the United States is committed to working with the international community to address these concerns, bearing in mind the fundamental need to ensure stability and security of the Internet's DNS.

ICANN is the appropriate technical manager of the Internet DNS. The United States continues to support the ongoing work of ICANN as the technical manager of the DNS and related technical operations and recognizes the progress it has made to date. The United States will continue to provide oversight so that ICANN maintains its focus and meets its core technical mission.

Dialogue related to Internet governance should continue in relevant multiple fora. Given the breadth of topics potentially encompassed under the rubric of Internet governance there is no one venue to appropriately address the subject in its entirety. While the United States recognizes that the current Internet system is working, we encourage an ongoing dialogue with all stakeholders around the world in the various fora as a way to facilitate discussion and to advance our shared interest in the ongoing robustness and dynamism of the Internet. In these fora, the United States will continue to support market-based approaches and private sector leadership in Internet development broadly.

[135] "I am writing you at this time to convey my concerns about security ramifications for future NATO operations if the European Union proceeds with Galileo satellite navigation services that would overlay spectrum of the Global Positioning System (GPS) military M-code signals.
Over the next several years, the U.S. plans a major modification to GPS to meet future military and civil requirements. One significant feature of the modernization is the spectral separation of the GPS military M-code signals from civil signals. Separating the signals will facilitate our ability to deny adversaries the

benefit of these space-based navigation services in a local theater of operations without negating the military use of the system.

In a recent meeting in the U.S., a European Commission (EC) delegation indicated that a Galileo Public Regulated Service (PRS) was being considered for the same spectrum planned for the modernized GPS M-code signals. The addition of any Galileo services in the same spectrum as the GPS M-code will significantly complicate our ability to ensure availability of critical military GPS services in a time of crisis or conflict and at the same time assure that adversary forces are denied similar capabilities. Additionally, I am concerned that it is intended that the Galileo PRS will have the features of the military signals of GPS. If the future PRS is actually intended to serve such a purpose, I do not believe the current civil forum being used by the EC provides the proper venue to fully assess the security implications.

I believe that acceptable solutions can be found and that we can avert potentially serious impacts to future alliance operations that rely on GPS. To find such solutions, however, I believe we need to identify and establish the proper forum to discuss the security ramifications of these future services. In this regard, I urge you to consider two actions. First, convey these security concerns to your Minister of Transport in advance of the 6 December EC meeting to review the Galileo mandate. In expressing these concerns, I believe it is in the interest of NATO to preclude future Galileo signal development in spectrum to be used by the GPS M-code. Second, inquire whether the EC intends to develop a Galileo PRS that will have military features and, if so, we must examine in an appropriate forum the security implications of the proposed system."

[136] EU-Commission Video: Galileo, The Countdown has Begun (27/12/2005 | REF :I-050006| 10:28) http://ec.europa.eu/avservices/vide o/video_prod_ en.cfm?type=detail&prodid=416.

137 Remarks as prepared for delivery by Dr. John Poindexter, Director, Information Awareness Office of DARPA, at DARPATech 2002 Conference, Anaheim, Calif., August 2, 2002 (Overview of the Information Awareness Office).

138 *Tag You're It: Privacy Implications of Radio Frequency Identification (RFID) Technology*, Ann Cavoukian, Ph.D. Information and Privacy Commissioner, Toronto, Ontario.

139 Steve Traiman, Tag, You're It! The EPC Tag Could Revolutionize the Retail Supply Chain, Retail Systems Reseller (November 2001).

140 "The New Network: Identify Any Object Anywhere Automatically," Dirk Heyman, Sun Microsystems, global head of life science and consumer product industries MIT Auto-ID Center. Cambridge, Massachusetts: Massachusetts Institute of technology, May 2002.

141 Formerly governed by the Uniform Code Council (UCC).

142 Formerly governed by the EAN International.

143 GS1 was formed when the Uniform Code Council (UCC) and the Electronic Commerce Council of Canada (ECCC) joined EAN International. UCC has become GS1 US and ECCC has become GS1 Canada. GS1's headquarters are located in Brussels, Belgium and Lawrenceville, New Jersey.

144 This is referred to as the "Sunrise Date."

145 EPCglobal, Inc.

146 www.wikipedia.org.

147 Computers in the United States and Canada were right-justified and added two leading digits to accommodate point-of-sale capabilities for EAN-13 and the future 14-digit numbers.

148 2d PDF 417.


## CHAPTER FOURTEEN:

149 Galileo's father, Vincenzo Galilei, is quoted as saying, *"It appears to me that those who rely simply on the weight of authority to prove any assertion, without searching out the arguments to support it, act absurdly. I wish to question freely and to answer freely without any sort of adulation. That well becomes any who are sincere in the search for truth."* See *Galileo, a Life*, James Reston, Jr., HarperCollins.

150 GPS is a space-based dual use radio-navigation system that is operated for the Government of the United States by the U.S. Air Force. The U.S. Government provides two levels of GPS service. The Precise Positioning Service (PPS) provides full system accuracy to designated users. The Standard Positioning Service (SPS) provides accurate positioning to all users. The Standard Positioning Service (SPS) was originally designed to provide civil users with a less accurate positioning capability than PPS through the use of a technique known as Selective Availability (SA). On May 1, 2000, President Bill Clinton directed the U.S. Department of Defense (DoD) to discontinue the use of SA effective midnight May 1, 2000. The GPS has three major segments: space, control, and user.

151 GLONASS consists (like other GNSS) of the ground segment, space segment and user receivers (user segment). The space-based positioning and navigation system provides worldwide, all weather, passive, three-dimensional position, velocity, and time data.

[152] *Space Diplomacy,* Foreign Affairs, by David Braunschvig, Richard L. Garwin, and Jeremy C. Marwell; published by the Council on Foreign Relations, July/August 2003.

[153] *Tag You're It: Privacy Implications of Radio Frequency Identification (RFID) Technology,* Ann Cavoukian, Ph.D. Information and Privacy Commissioner, Toronto, Ontario, page 15

[154] "Radio Frequency Identification—RFID A basic primer," white paper by Association for Automatic Identification and Mobility (AIM, Inc.), http://www.aimglobal.org/.

[155] Id.

[156] Id.

[157] Id.

[158] Id

[159] David Streitfeld; "A Chip ID That's Only Skin-Deep;" Los Angeles Times; published December 19, 2001; Start Page: A.1.

[160] Written guidance from the U.S. Food and Drug Administration (FDA) that the chip is not considered a "regulated medical device."

[161] "Company to Sell Implantable Chip;" Associated Press on washingtonpost.com; published April 4, 2002.

[162] "VeriChip Receives Favorable FDA Guidance: Sales, Marketing and Distribution of VeriChip to Begin in the United States;" published April 4, 2002; www.allbusiness.com.

[163] *The European Dream,* by Jeremy Rifkin, Penguin Group (USA) Inc. 2004 (pages 201-202).

[164] March 25, 1957

[165] Grant R. Jeffrey, *The Signature of God*, 1996, pp. 190-191.

[166] Daniel 9:26

[167] The Council for the EU is a legislative body. It is the main decision-making body for the EU. It coordinates economic policies, possesses budgetary authority and concludes international agreements.

[168] The Parliament for the EU is also a Legislative body. It maintains political supervision over all the EU countries. It maintains Democratic supervision over the EU Commission and it also possesses budgetary authority.

[169] The Commission for the EU is an executive body. It presents legislative proposals, implements legislation and negotiates international agreements.

[170] www.wikipedia.org.

[171] International Monetary Fund (IMF) http://www.imf.org/external/European Union, (Gross Domestic Product in U.S. dollars) for 2003-11,273.138, 2004-12,980.129, 2005-13,502.800, 2006-14,205.938, 2007-15,183.404 (in billions). 34 percent increase in four years.

[172] Blue Tower, Avenue Louise, 326, BE 1050 Brussels, Belgium.

[173] Rue de la Loi, 175 B-1048 Bruxelles, Belgium.

[174] The EU Parliament holds its sessions in Brussels, Belgium, Rue Wiertz 60, Wiertzstraat 60, B-1047 Bruxelles, Belgium.(the "seat" of the European Parliament is Strasbourg).

[175] EU Commission locations in Belgium include; (1) Archimède 73, rue Archimède, 73, 1000—Bruxelles, (2) Arlon 88 (SCAN), rue d' Arlon, 88, 1040—Bruxelles, (3) Belliard 28, rue Belliard, 28, 1040—Bruxelles, (4) Belliard 100, rue Belliard, 100, 1040—Bruxelles, (5) Belliard 232, rue Breydel, 4, 1040—Bruxelles, (6) Berlaymont, rue de la Loi, 200, 1040—Bruxelles, (7) Breydel 2, avenue d'Auderghem, 19, 1040—Bruxelles, (8) Breydel, avenue d'Auderghem, 45, 1040—Bruxelles, (9) Cortenberg 80, avenue de Cortenbergh, 80, 1000—Bruxelles, (10) Cortenberg 100, avenue de Cortenbergh, 100, 1000—Bruxelles, (11) Cortenberg 107, avenue de Cortenbergh, 107, 1000—Bruxelles, (12) Centre Albert Borschette, rue Froissart, 36, 1040—Bruxelles, (13) Champ de Mars, rue de Champ de Mars, 21, 1050—Bruxelles, (14) Charlemagne, rue de la Loi, 170, 1040—Bruxelles, (15) Crèche Clovis, boulevard Clovis, 75, 1000—Bruxelles, (16) Cour Saint-Michel 1, rue Père de Deken, 23, 1040—Bruxelles, (17) Cour Saint-Michel 2, avenue de Tervuren, 41, 1040—Bruxelles, (18) Demot 24, rue Demot, 24, 1040—Bruxelles, (19) Demot 28, rue Demot, 28, 1040—Bruxelles, (20) Froissart 101, rue Froissart, 101, 1040—Bruxelles, (21) Genève 8, rue de Genève, 6-8, 1140—Bruxelles, (22) Guimard, rue Guimard, 10, 1040—Bruxelles, (23) IMCO, avenue de Cortenbergh, 6, 1040—Bruxelles, (24) Joseph II 27, rue Joseph II, 27, 1000—Bruxelles, (25) Joseph II 30, rue Joseph II, 30, 1000—Bruxelles, (26) Joseph II 37, rue Joseph II, 37, 1000—Bruxelles, (27) Joseph II 54, Rue Joseph II, 54, 1000—Bruxelles, (28) Joseph II 70, rue Joseph II, 70, 1000—Bruxelles, (29) Joseph II 79, Rue Joseph II, 79, 1000—Bruxelles, (30) Joseph II 99, rue Joseph II, 99, 1000—Bruxelles, (31) Loi 41, rue de la Loi, 41, 1040—Bruxelles, (32) Loi 86, rue de la Loi, 86, 1040—Bruxelles, (33) Loi 102, rue de la Loi, 102, 1040—Bruxelles, (34) Loi 130, rue de la Loi, 130, 1040—Bruxelles, (35) Luxembourg 46, (36) rue de Luxembourg, 46, 1050—Bruxelles, (37) Montoyer 34, rue Montoyer, 34, 1000—Bruxelles, (38) Montoyer 51, rue Montoyer, 51, 1000—Bruxelles, (39) Montoyer 59, rue Montoyer, 59, 1000—Bruxelles, (40) Nerviens 105, avenue des Nerviens, 105, 1040—Bruxelles, (41) Crèche Palmerston, avenue Palmerston, 6/14, 1000—Bruxelles, (42) InfEuropa

Schuman 14, rue archimede, 1, 1000—Bruxelles, (43) Science 11, rue de la Science, 11, 1040—Bruxelles, (44) Science 15, rue de la Science, 15, 1040—Bruxelles, (45) Science 27 (SCAN), rue de la Science, 27, 1040—Bruxelles, (46) Science 29 (SCAN), rue de la Science, 29, 1040—Bruxelles, (47) Square de Meeûs, square de Meeûs, 8, 1050—Bruxelles, (48) SPA2—Pavillon, rue de Spa, 2, 1000—Bruxelles, (49) Spa 3, rue de Spa,3, 1000—Bruxelles, (50) Van Maerlant 2, rue Van Maerlant, 2, 1040—Bruxelles, (51) Couvent Van Maerlant, rue Van Maerlant, 18, 1040—Bruxelles, (52) Garderie Wilson, rue Wilson, 16, 1000—Bruxelles.

[176] "Council on Foreign Affairs": publication Foreign Affairs, July/August 2003 Space Diplomacy, by David Braunschvig, Richard L. Garwin, and Jeremy C. Marwell.

[177] Id.

[178] EU-Commission Video: "Galileo, The Countdown has Begun" (27/12/2005 | REF :I-050006| 10:28) http://ec.europa.eu/avservices/video/video_prod_en.cfm?type=detail&prodid=416.

[179] http://www.gpsworld.com/gpsworld/static/staticHtml.jsp?id=97978.

[180] EU-Commission Video: Galileo, The European Initiative, March 2002 [6:51] http://ec.europa.eu/dgs/energy_transport/galileo/video/index_en.htm.

[181] EU-Commission Video: Galileo, The Countdown has Begun (27/12/2005 | REF:I-050006| 10:28)http://ec.europa.eu/avservices/video/video_prod_en.cfm?type=detail&prodid=416.

[182] Jack Z. Smith, Staff Writer, Fort Worth Star-Telegram, January 28, 2005

[183] The Texas Department of Transportation, Tomorrow's Transportation System, Strategic Plan 2005-2009.

[184] Jack Z. Smith, Staff Writer,Fort Worth Star-Telegram, January 28, 2005.

[185] Steve Pustelnyk, Director of Communications, Central Texas Regional Mobility Authority
Interview with Community Impact Newspaper (April 2008) Vol. 3, Issue 8
http://impactnews.com/leander-cedar-park/local-news/142-news/681-toll-183a-one-year-later.

[186] Plaza Manuel Gómez Moreno 2, Edificio Alfredo Mahou 28020, Madrid, Spain.

[187] http://www.esa.int/esaNA/SEMVQ10DU8E_galileo_0.html.
http://www.esa.int/esaNA/SEMKMQWO4HD_egnos_0.html.
http://www.esa.int/esaNA/ESAWW20VMOC_index_0.html.

## CHAPTER FIFTEEN:

[188] http://www.korteks.com/Applications/Applications_TOC.htm.
http://www.activewaveinc.com/applications_parking_lots.php.
http://www.telecomspace.com/wirelessnw-rfid.html.

[189] "Who Will Control the Internet?" by Kenneth Neil Cukier, Foreign Affairs, published by the Council on Foreign Affairs November/December 2005, Vol 84, Number 6.

# CHAPTER SIXTEEN:

190   Charles R. Swindoll, Insight for Living, *Solomon: A Plea for Godliness*, January 6-8, 2009.

191   Charles R. Swindoll, Insight for Living, *Deuteronomy: Remember, Remember*, June23-27, 2011.

192   <u>Mark 1:15 LEB</u>: *"The time has come," he said. "The kingdom of God has come near. **Repent and believe** the good news!"*

# GLOSSARY

**3-Hydroxyanthranilic Acid:** (3HAA) is an intermediate in the metabolism of tryptophan.

**Counter Intelligence:** espionage undertaken to detect and counteract enemy espionage.

**Coup d'état:** forcefuloverthrow of the existing power structure; the sudden overthrow of a government by a usually small group of persons in or previously in positions of authority.

**De facto:** actual, by definition.

**Electronic Product Code:** (EPC) The EPC was the creation of the MITAuto-ID Center, a consortium of over 120 global corporations and university labs. EPC identifiers were designed to identify each item manufactured, as opposed to just the manufacturer and class of products, as bar codes do today. The EPC system is currently managed by EPCglobal, Inc., a subsidiary of GS1. The specifications for the EPC identifiers can be found in the EPCglobal, Inc. The EPC is one of the industrial standards for global RFID usage, and a core element of the EPCglobal Network, an architecture of open standards developed by the GS1 EPCglobal community. Most currently deployed EPC RFID tags comply with ISO/IEC 18000-6C for the RFID air interface standard.

**I Ching:** A Chinese book of ancient origin consisting of 64 interrelated hexagrams along with commentaries attributed to Confucius. The hexagrams, originally used for divination, embody Taoist philosophy by describing all nature and human endeavor in terms of the interaction of yin and yang. Also called the *Book of Changes*.

**Modus Operandi:** (M.O.) mode of operating or way of working.

**Radio Frequency Identification:** (RFID) data collection technology that uses electronic tags for storing data. The tag, also known as an "electronic label," "transponder" or "code plate," is made up of an RFID chip attached to an antenna. Transmitting in the kilohertz, megahertz and gigahertz ranges, tags may be battery-powered or derive their power from the RF waves coming from the reader. Like bar codes, RFID tags identify items. However, unlike bar codes, which must be in close proximity and line of sight to the scanner for reading, RFID tags do not require line of sight and can be embedded within packages.

**Sunrise Date:** industry initiative whereby the USA and Canada businesses must be capable of scanning the 8-digit and 13-digit EAN codes at the point-of-sale by January 1, 2005.

**Web Bot Computer:** refers to an internet bot software program that is claimed to be able to predict future events by tracking keywords entered on the Internet. It was created in 1997, originally to predict stock market trends. The creator of the Web Bot Project, Clif High, keeps the technology and algorithms largely secret and sells the predictions via the website.

# RESOURCES

WWW.GIVE-AN-ANSWER.COM

# BIBLIOGRAPHY

"*Third Millennium Teens, Research on the Minds, Hearts and Souls of America's Teenagers,*"Barna Research Group, Ltd., 1999

"The Real ID Act and the Public Administration of Global Radio Frequency Identification (RFID) Policies," by Bart Bevers, *International In-House Council Journal*, Vol. 2, No. 5, Autumn 2008, 708-725.

*Fostering Ethics and Accountability in the Public-Sector Workplace,* by Bart Bevers, Strategic Public Management Best Practices from Government and Nonprofit Organizations (Howard R. Balanoff & Warren Master eds., 2010).

*The Millennium,* by Lorraine Boettner [Nutley, N.J.: Presbyterian and Reformed, 1957].

"*Berlusconi New Italian Premier Indictments, Fickle Allies Are Potential Pitfalls for New PM*", by Richard Boudreaux, The Los Angeles Times, May 15, 2001. (Volume 121, Number 26).

*Space Diplomacy,* Foreign Affairs Magazine, by <u>David Braunschvig</u>, <u>Richard L. Garwin</u>, and <u>Jeremy C. Marwell</u>; published by the Council on Foreign Relations, July/August 2003.

"Silvio Berlusconi, self-styled man of the people," by Francesca Caferri, CNN Italy, 2001.

"Italy's Houdini poised to pull off his greatest trick," by Rory Carroll, The Guardian International, Saturday December 16, 2000.

*Tag You're It: Privacy Implications of Radio Frequency Identification (RFID) Technology,* Ann Cavoukian, Ph.D. Information and Privacy Commissioner, Toronto, Ontario.

"Who Will Control the Internet?" by Kenneth Neil Cukier, Foreign Affairs, published by the Council on Foreign Affairs November/December 2005, Vol 84, Number 6.

"Commentary: Berlusconi's Accidental Gift to Bin Laden", Gail Edmondson, *BusinessWeek<u>, October 22, 2001.</u>*

"First Among Billionaires,"James Fox, *The Guardian,* September 28, 2002.

"The New Network: Identify Any Object Anywhere Automatically,"Dirk Heyman, Sun Microsystems, global head of life science and consumer product industries MIT Auto-ID Center. Cambridge, Massachusetts: Massachusetts Institute of Technology, May 2002.

*The Signature of God,* Grant R. Jeffrey, (W. Publishing Group, a Division of Thomas Nelson, Inc. 1998).

"Overview of the Information Awareness Office," remarks as prepared for delivery by Dr. John Poindexter, Director,

Information Awareness Office of DARPA, at DARPATech 2002 Conference, Anaheim, Calif., August 2, 2002.

*Galileo, a Life*, James Reston, Jr., HarperCollins Publishers, 1994.

*The European Dream*, by Jeremy Rifkin. Penguin Group (USA) Inc. 2004.

*Basic Theology*, by Charles Ryrie, Moody Press [6th edition 1988].

"Italy's Berlusconi and his 'House of Freedoms'—a new dimension in the development of the right wing in Europe," by Peter Schwarz, *World Socialist We Site*, May 7, 2001.

Jack Z. Smith, Staff Writer, *Fort Worth Star-Telegram*, January 28, 2005.

"A Chip ID That's Only Skin-Deep;" David Streitfeld; *Los Angeles Times*; published December 19, 2001.

*Hebrew and Chaldee Dictionary, The Hebrew-Greek Key Study Bible* (AMG Publishers, 1990). James Strong, S.T.D., L.L.D.

"The Texas Department of Transportation, Tomorrow's Transportation System, Strategic Plan," 2005-2009.

"Tag, You're It! The EPC Tag Could Revolutionize the Retail Supply Chain," Steve Traiman, *Retail Systems Reseller* (November 2001).

*The Bible Knowledge Commentary*, John F. Walvoord and Roy B. Zuck, (Colorado Springs, CO, Cook Communications Ministries 2000).

"Silvio Berlusconi's Report Card," Philip Willan, *The Guardian*, May 15, 2002.

"Fans of Berlusconi Reveal Nobel Intent," Philip Willan, *The Guardian*, September 4, 2002.

"Mirth and Anger at Berlusconi 'Miracle,'" BBC World News, November 15, 2000, by David Willey in Rome.

"Italian boycott over euro price hikes," BBC News, David Willey, July 5, 2002.

*The American Heritage Dictionary,* Houghton Mifflin Company, 1982 (2nd College Edition).

"Radio Frequency Identification—RFID A Basic Primer," white paper by Association for Automatic Identification and Mobility, AIM, Inc.

"VeriChip Receives Favorable FDA Guidance: Sales, Marketing and Distribution of VeriChip to Begin in the United States," published April 4, 2002; www.allbusiness.com.

"Silvio Berlusconi," Askmen.com, March 9, 2003.
*Community Impact Newspaper,* Round Rock, Texas (April 2008) Vol. 3, Issue 8.

*The Palestine Chronicle*, March 17, 2002.
*U.S. Department of Commerce: National Telecommunications and Information Administration,* June 30, 2005.